Mrs. Latham leaned wearily back against the draining board. "Shelley, sometimes I don't know what to do with you." Shelley stared at the ceiling. Sometimes she didn't know what to do about her mother. Then she was surprised to hear her own voice telling her mother, "Send me to California to live with the Michies." Shelley knew as she spoke that she meant what she said. It would be exciting to spend a winter in California, to wear a dirty old slicker if she felt like it, to go to a different school, to meet new people—and not go out with Jack. Let Rosemary or some other girl have him. Shelley wouldn't care. She was going to California and something wonderful and new would surely happen.

BEVERLY CLEARY grew up in Portland, Oregon, and was graduated from the University of California at Berkeley and the School of Librarianship at the University of Washington at Seattle. She is the author of several award-winning books for children and teen-agers, including *Fifteen* (available in a Laurel-Leaf edition). Mrs. Cleary currently lives in California with her husband.

Chapter 1

One Saturday morning early in September Shelley Latham sat at the breakfast table with her mother and father. Her mother was reading the women's page of the morning paper while her father read the editorial section. There were dahlias in the center of the table and linen mats under each plate; the electric coffeepot gleamed in a ray of morning sunlight. It was a peaceful scene, apparently no different from any other Saturday morning breakfast at the Lathams', but this morning there was a difference, invisible but real. This morning Shelley was plotting.

Outside Shelley heard the rasp of a dry leaf scudding along the driveway. The sound meant the season was changing, and she intended to make her life change with it. That was what made the start of a new high-school year exciting—the possibility that this time things could be different. New school clothes, a change of locker partners, a new boy across the aisle in English class, even the autumn air, crisp and shining—all these could make a big difference in a girl's life.

And Shelley had made up her mind that this year, her junior year, there was going to be a difference. For one thing, she was no longer going to go steady with Jack. How she would break off she did not know, but it would be soon, this very day perhaps.

But before she could do anything about Jack, Shelley had another problem to settle and the time to do it was now. She looked at her mother, who was innocently eating a soft-boiled egg, and made up her mind to be firm from the very start.

"Shelley, here's an advertisement for a school dress that would be pretty on you," remarked the unsuspecting Mrs. Latham. "A blue wool-and-rabbit hair with a full skirt."

Shelley was not going to lose sight of her goal. Anyway, she did not want a dress like that for school. She preferred sweaters and skirts such as all the other girls wore. "Mother, I am going downtown this afternoon to buy my slicker," Shelley stated. It was always best to be definite about a controversial subject and to introduce it when her father was present. "School starts Tuesday and I might need it," she explained logically, although her reason for wanting the slicker was not logical at all. She did not know why she wanted a slicker. She only knew that owning one was important and somehow might help make her year different.

"Oh, Shelley, you don't really want one of those awful slickers," remarked Mrs. Latham as she used her napkin to wipe up some pollen that had fallen from the dahlias to the gleaming surface of the mahogany table.

Shelley could not help smiling, because this was exactly what she had expected her mother to say. I'll put it on my list, she thought. If she ever had a sixteen-year-old daughter who wanted a slicker, she would not refer to it as "one of those awful slickers."

Shelley's list, now imaginary, had begun when she was twelve, going-on-thirteen. At that time she had printed on the outside of an envelope: "To be read by me if I ever have a twelve-year-old daughter." On a sheet of paper she had written:

"1. I will let her read in bed all she wants without telling her she will ruin her eyes.

"2. I will not tell my friends embarrassing things that happen to her and laugh.

"3. I will not hang crummy old paper chains on the Christmas tree just because she made them when she was a little girl."

A year later Shelley, touched that her mother had treasured the faded paper chains because she had once worked so hard to make them with colored paper and library paste, crossed the third item off the list. A few months ago when she had been going steady with Jack for some time, she had written in its place: "3. I will not show her baby pictures to boys who come to see her." And soon after that Shelley decided the list was childish and tore it up. But the habit persisted, the list becoming imaginary and the items half-forgotten as soon as Shelley noted them.

The conversation about the purchase of the slicker was postponed by a letter that dropped through the slot in the front door and slid across the polished floor. Shelley picked up the letter and glanced at the return address, 613 N. Mirage Avenue, San Sebastian, California—an address that never failed to delight her. She always wondered if there was a South Mirage, too, and if both parts of the avenue might not someday disappear because they were named for something that was not real at all, but only an illusion of the eye. "It's from your college roommate," she said, as she handed the letter to her mother.

Mrs. Latham tore open the envelope and began to read. "Honestly, if that isn't just like Mavis," she remarked after a moment, as she paused to fill her cup from the electric coffeepot.

"What's like Mavis?" asked Shelley, who had always been interested in her mother's former roommate. Mavis, Shelley remembered her mother's telling her, had brought a mounted deer head—the head of a six-point buck—to school to decorate their small room in the dormitory of the teachers' college.

"Listen to this," said Mrs. Latham, and began to read. " 'Why don't you send Shelley down here for the winter? We have an excellent high school in San Sebastian and classes do not start until the day after Admission Day. We have plenty of room and it might be fun for her to spend a winter in California. I know we would enjoy having her and I am sure that another girl in the house would be a good experience for Katie, who has reached a difficult age.' " Mrs. Latham put down the letter. "That's just like Mavis—always suggesting something impractical on the spur of the moment. As if we could pack Shelley up and send her over a thousand miles away on a few days' notice!"

Of course she could never pack up and go to school over a thousand miles away. Shelley felt there was no point in even discussing it. She would finish high school and go to the University just like everyone else. Anyway, she did not want to be a good experience for a girl who had reached a difficult age, even though she was curious to know what a difficult age for a girl like Katie would be. Six years before, Tom and Mavis Michie with their children, Luke and Katie, had visited the Lathams for three days during the Rose Festival. Shelley had been expected to entertain Katie, but after half a day she had looked forward to the younger girl's departure. Katie had also been at a difficult stage six years ago.

"What's Admission Day?" Shelley asked idly.

"I don't know," answered Mrs. Latham, returning the letter to the envelope, because she was equally sure there was no reason to discuss Shelley's going to California. "I suppose it is some California holiday."

"Admission Day is the ninth of September, the day California was admitted to the Union," explained Shelley's father, looking up from the editorials. Mr. Latham had a way of knowing the answers to unexpected questions.

What a nice thing to celebrate, thought Shelley, wondering why Oregon did not have a similar holiday. Perhaps it was because California's history of Spanish settlers, earthquakes, and the gold rush had always seemed so much more colorful than Oregon's traditional history of hardy pioneers toiling with their hands to the plow.

"What else does Mavis say?" asked Shelley's father.

"Tom expects to have more students in his math class this year and hopes to coach a winning basketball team," answered Mrs. Latham. "They had a record crop from their orange grove last winter. Luke has managed to get hold of an old wreck of a motorcycle that he hopes to get into working order—Mavis says she would be worried except that it is so dilapidated that she is sure it never will run—and Katie is doing very well with her piano lessons if only she would practice."

"A motorcycle! It doesn't seem possible that Luke is that old," observed Mr. Latham. "Let's see, how old was he that time they visited us?"

"Katie was seven, Luke was nine, and I was ten, so that makes Katie thirteen and Luke fifteen," answered Shelley. "I'll never forget how I was supposed to entertain Katie and how awful she was. She tried to chin herself on the towel racks in the bathroom and pulled them right out of the wall."

"And Shelley," said Mrs. Latham, laughing, "do you remember how your father was fit to be tied when she used his favorite pipe to blow soap bubbles?"

Shelley giggled. "And he didn't say a thing, but the way he *looked* . . . ." Shelley and her mother went off into a gale of laughter.

"Luke was easy enough to entertain. I remember he spent all his time tinkering with an old alarm clock, but Katie certainly was a handful." Mrs. Latham laid the letter beside the place mat in front of her and took a sip of coffee.

Because the conversation about the Michies seemed to be over, Shelley felt this was the moment to mention the slicker once more. "Mother, I'll have to go downtown this afternoon to buy my slicker," she stated a second time, trying not to sound anxious. "The stores will be closed Monday because of Labor Day and school starts Tuesday."

"Shelley, I saw the prettiest raincoat the other day," said Mrs. Latham. "It was pink with a black velveteen collar and had a little hat with a velveteen button on top—"

"Pink!" exclaimed Shelley with distaste. "But Mother, I don't want a pink raincoat with a velveteen collar. You *know* I want a plain ordinary everyday yellow slicker and a plain ordinary everyday hat to match."

"And to look just like that boy on the label of a can of sardines," Mrs. Latham told her daughter. "Shelley dear, yellow is not becoming to you, and the girls who wear those slickers always look so sloppy."

"But Mother, if I wore a pink raincoat with a velveteen collar to school everyone would think I was too dressed up or something," said Shelley stubbornly. "I want a slicker."

"Oh, Shelley," said Mrs. Latham impatiently. "Do you want to be one of a bunch of sheep?"

"Yes," answered Shelley flatly.

Mr. Latham looked up from his paper, glanced at Shelley and then at his wife, frowned, and resumed his reading.

"Those slickers get so dirty and there is no way to clean them. And they get torn and shabby in no time at all," Mrs. Latham pointed out. "They really aren't practical."

"But a slicker isn't—well, *mellow* until it gets dirty," Shelley tried to explain.

Mrs. Latham laughed. "Shelley, I don't know where you girls get such ideas."

"I don't care, Mother," said Shelley, resenting her mother's amusement. "It's what all the girls wear and it's what I want. And besides, it's my own money."

"Oh, well, there is really no hurry," said Mrs. Latham lightly, as she rose to clear the table. "We've had such a wet summer we're bound to have some nice weather this fall."

The trouble with Mother, thought Shelley, as she carried her plate into the kitchen and dropped a scrap of toast into the Disposall, is that she doesn't understand. And the importance of a slicker was so hard to explain. A dirty yellow slicker, mended with adhesive tape and covered with names in ink—the right names, of course—was the smartest thing a girl could wear to school. It showed a girl was . . . well, Shelley was not quite sure what wearing a shabby slicker showed. It was one of those things that was difficult to put into words, but it was *important*. Couldn't her mother see that?

"Is Jack coming over this evening?" Mrs. Latham asked, pointedly changing the subject while she and Shelley washed and wiped the breakfast dishes.

"I suppose so," said Shelley, deciding to let the question of the slicker drop for the time being. "He always does. At least, I am expecting him to phone after a while." And ask if anything exciting had happened, even though she had seen him only the night before. Jack always asked if anything exciting had happened just as he always said *Gesundheit* if she sneezed. Always. If she sneezed twice, he said *Gesundheit* twice. Not that Shelley sneezed any more than anyone else. It was just that she had seen so much of Jack that she felt she knew what he was going to say before he said it.

"He's such a nice boy," said Mrs. Latham comfortably. "I never worry when you are out with Jack."

"I know." There was wistfulness in Shelley's voice, not because she wanted to worry her mother, but because she was so tired of Jack.

Jack was not the first boy Shelley had known. First there had been Peter, who had taken her to the Girls' League Show at school and to a movie. There had been nothing wrong with Peter, really, but both he and Shelley were so uncertain and had such difficulty finding anything to talk about that they could not feel comfortable in one another's company.

Next came Roger, from Shelley's Latin class, who took her to her first school dance. Shelley liked Roger even if he did have large ears and wore glasses. He solved the problem of dancing by repeating a set pattern of steps he had learned in his dancing class. Since the pattern did not vary, Shelley quickly learned to do a reverse version of his steps instead of trying to follow—something that she could not do very well. Then Roger suggested that they speak as much as possible in Latin. Shelley thought this was fun as well as a solution to the problem of something to talk about. She used her ingenuity and limited Latin to make such remarks as "The floor of the gymnasium is divided into three parts." When another couple bumped into them, she produced two complete sentences: "The boy and girl are not our friends. They are bad." She and Roger both thought this extremely funny.

When Mrs. Latham asked Shelley about the dance, Shelley described her evening. Mrs. Latham smiled and said, "I'm glad you had a good time, dear." Then she said thoughtfully, "Isn't it too bad you don't have some really nice-looking boy to take you to school affairs?"

Not long after that Shelley came home from school one warm afternoon when the front door was open and heard her mother talking to a friend on the telephone. "Yes, Shelley seemed to have a good time at the dance," Mrs. Latham was saying. "It was her first dance, you know, but I could hardly keep my face straight when she was telling me about it. She and Roger spoke *Latin*—can you imagine, at a *dance*? . . . I don't know exactly what they found to say, but Shelley did mention that she said, 'The floor of the gymnasium is divided into three parts,' the way Caesar said all Gaul is divided into three parts, and she seemed quite proud of it." Mrs. Latham shared a laugh with her friend before she continued, "Poor child. He is so homely. I do wish—"

Shelley's rickety confidence collapsed. Her evening with Roger now seemed ridiculous, laid waste, as the old Romans would have said, by her mother's account to a friend. But Mother did not mean me to hear, Shelley tried to tell herself, and she would have been dreadfully upset if she knew I had overheard the conversation. But Shelley could not, no matter how hard she tried, escape the fact that she *had* overheard and that her feelings had been hurt. After that she saw

Roger through her mother's eyes, as a homely, rather ridiculous boy.

Jack was next. Shelley had liked Jack the first time he asked her for a date and her mother liked him too. Shelley liked him the second and the third time she went out with him, but by the fourth date, when everyone assumed they were going steady, Shelley found she did not like Jack nearly so much as she thought she had. And then it was too late. Now she wished some other girl would have to listen to him say, "Penny for your thoughts," every time there was a lull in the conversation.

"So many girls don't have anybody," Mrs. Latham was saying as she rinsed the electric coffeepot, "but you have a good-looking boy with nice manners who comes from a good family."

For the first time that morning Shelley faltered in her determination. Her mother was right. So many girls stayed home on Saturday night and pretended to have fun playing records or looking at television. So many girls tried to make one date sound like half-a-dozen when they talked to one another at school. Lots of girls would be eager to go out with Jack. Even Rosemary, her best friend. Everybody said that Shelley was so lucky to have such a nice boy to take her places, that she and Jack made a cute couple (cute couple—she detested the phrase!) . . . and where would she find another boy to take his place? All the boys a girl would like to know were either going steady or they were the exasperating kind who were more interested in sports or studies than dates.

"I'm going to cut some roses for the table," said Mrs. Latham, removing her apron. "Maybe you would like to arrange them."

"All right, Mother," agreed Shelley, who enjoyed flower arranging. She went into her room and began to make her bed. She tossed her pillows onto a chair and smoothed the sheets, and while she worked she carried on a mental conversation. Good-by, Jack . . . no, I'm not mad at you—I'm just not going out with you any more. In her imagination, while she pulled up the soft blue blankets, Jack answered, But golly, Shelley . . . Jack always said, But golly, Shelley, when she said something that worried him. Then she would say—what? I'm sorry, Jack, but you bore me stiff? No, a girl could not say that to a boy who had, in his own way, tried to give her a good time. Shelley pulled up the quilted chintz spread. There must be a way out. There had to be and soon, too. If she were seen with Jack during the first few days of school, everyone would assume she did not want to go out with any other boy and then her junior year would be just like her sophomore year—a series of Saturday nights each like the one before and the one that lay ahead.

"Here are the roses," Mrs. Latham called out from the kitchen.

"All right, Mother." Shelley went into the kitchen, where she found a tangle of roses on the draining board. She began to strip the lower leaves from the stems and drop them into the Disposall. The roses were among the last that would bloom that season and the colors, pink and red, yellow and white, showed that her mother had cut most of the blooms from the bushes to have enough for the table. Because she had so many colors to work with, Shelley decided to make a bouquet rather than a formal arrangement. She found a blue bowl and a frog in the cupboard and was sorting out the roses with the longest stems for the center of the bouquet when the doorbell rang.

"It must be the parcel service," remarked Mrs. Latham and went to the door. She returned in a moment with a suit box, which she laid on the draining board while she snipped the cord with her garden shears. She removed the lid, pushed aside the tissue paper, and lifted out a pink raincoat with a black velveteen collar.

"Mother!" cried Shelley in dismay.

"A surprise for you," announced Mrs. Latham gaily.

"But Mother—" protested Shelley.

"Now Shelley," said Mrs. Latham comfortably, "be sensible."

"I don't want to be sensible," cried Shelley, "I want a yellow slicker. You knew I wanted a slicker. I saved my money for it."

"But Shelley, this will be so becoming to you," said Mrs. Latham. "You look so sweet in pink."

Shelley enunciated with exaggerated distinctness. "Mother, I do not want to look sweet." Sweet! How old did her mother think she was, anyway? Six instead of sixteen?

"Now Shelley," said Mrs. Latham in what Shelley recognized as her subject-is-closed voice, "I don't want my daughter wearing a sloppy old slicker. Your father will pay for this and you can use your money for something else. A pretty new skirt perhaps."

But Shelley was not willing to let the subject be closed. She did not want a pretty skirt. She wanted a yellow slicker. An ugly yellow slicker. A slicker patched with adhesive tape. Rebellion mounted within her. She was being silly and childish and she knew it, but she had her heart set on that slicker, she had saved her money, and her mother had no right—

Shelley was frightened. What if she did not find the courage to tell Jack she did not want to go out with him again? And what if she wore the pink raincoat her mother had selected? Then nothing would be different after all. She felt cornered, desperate.

Then, feeling as if she had been building up to this moment for a long time, Shelley knew she had to do something that very instant to relieve her feelings. She looked wildly around the kitchen, snatched the roses from the draining board, and ignoring the thorns that scratched her hands, she stuffed the blooms into the Disposall, turned on the water, flipped the switch that started the motor and stood with her back to her mother, her fingers gripping the edge of the sink, and listened with savage pleasure while the angry jaws of the Disposall chewed the roses, petals, leaves, and stems to bits.

When the last shred of the roses was noisily ground up and washed away, Shelley stopped the motor and turned off the water. Then, taking a deep breath, she whirled around and faced her mother.

This time it was Mrs. Latham who was angry. Angry and shocked. "Shelley Latham!" she exclaimed. "Roses in the Disposall!"

Shelley looked defiant—more defiant than she felt, because she, too, was shocked at what she had done.

"Really, Shelley—" began Mrs. Latham and stopped. She did not know what to say.

Shelley remained silent. They faced one another, mother and daughter, one puzzled and hurt, the other stubborn and rebellious.

"What's going on here anyway?" asked Shelley's father, entering from the living room, the morning paper still in his hand.

"Shelley threw the roses into the Disposall," answered Mrs. Latham. "Perfectly good roses that I had just cut."

Shelley thought her father looked as if he were trying not to smile. I suppose it is funny, putting roses into the Disposall, she thought suddenly—funny to someone else. But she could not feel that there was anything funny about what she had done. She only knew that, for some reason she did not understand, she felt better because she had stuffed those roses into the Disposall, as if she had ground up some of her exasperation along with the petals. But this was something she did not know how to explain to her father.

"Shelley, sometimes I think I don't understand you any more," said Mrs. Latham with a sigh.

This did not surprise Shelley, who sometimes felt she no longer understood herself. "I just . . ." Shelley hesitated, not knowing how to justify her behavior to her father. "I guess . . . it is just that when I am bad I am horrid."

"I was only trying to do something for her own good," Mrs. Latham explained to Mr. Latham, "and suddenly she seized perfectly good roses, probably the last of the season, and stuffed them into the Disposall. *Destroyed* them. I can't understand it."

"But I don't want something done for my own good," protested Shelley. "That's the whole point."

"What was the argument about?" asked Mr. Latham. "I wasn't listening to this particular one."

"My slicker. Mother knew I had saved my money for a slicker," explained Shelley, "and she went and bought me a raincoat I didn't want."

"But that is no reason to grind up roses." Mrs. Latham leaned wearily back against the draining board. "Shelley, sometimes I don't know what to do with you."

Shelley stared at the ceiling. "Let me buy the slicker," was what she wanted to say, but instead she was surprised to hear her own voice telling her mother, "Send me to California."

"Now, Shelley," said Mrs. Latham, relenting. "Don't dramatize so. What you did was wrong, but we certainly don't intend to—to banish you over a few roses."

"But I want to go," answered Shelley, and knew as she spoke that she meant what she said. Even though it meant living in the same house with Katie, she wanted to go to California.

"But that is out of the question," protested Mrs. Latham. "As if we could send you all the way to California."

"Why is it impossible?" Mr. Latham asked. "A girl has to leave home sometime."

"Of course," agreed Mrs. Latham, "but there is plenty of time for that when she is ready for college. After all, Shelley is only sixteen and young for her age at that." Mrs. Latham acted as if there was nothing more to say on the subject. Briskly she set the blue bowl and the frog back in the cupboard and shut the door.

"Leaving home and having the opportunity to make a few mistakes is a good way for a girl to grow up," persisted Mr. Latham. "And this looks like a splendid opportunity for a girl who has never been more than a couple of hundred miles from home."

Shelley carefully examined a scratch on her forefinger. It was difficult to believe that her father could be serious, but it would be exciting to spend a winter in California, to wear a dirty old slicker if she felt like it, to go to a different school, and see some of the country, and meet new people—and not go out with Jack. Let Rosemary or some other girl have him. She wouldn't care, not when she was in California. What was it like down there in California, where history was so colorful and oranges came from trees instead of bins at the supermarket?

"Send our little girl so far away to live with someone else's family?" Mrs. Latham's voice expressed disbelief. "You can't really mean it."

Mr. Latham continued as if his wife had not spoken. "After all, Shelley is an only child and the experience of living with a larger family should be good for her."

Shelley considered this. She had always liked being an only child and had felt sorry for some of her friends who sometimes had to go without new clothes because of the expense of keeping an older brother or sister in college, or who had to baby-sit with younger brothers or sisters. It did not matter. Even if she had to baby-sit with Katie, she still wanted to go to California.

"But I couldn't bear to let her go so far," said Shelley's mother.

"I think she should go," Mr. Latham stated flatly.

"Daddy!" cried Shelley, while Mrs. Latham looked at her husband in silence.

"She may not have another chance like this." Mr. Latham went on as if Shelley was not listening. "When she is ready for college we won't be able to send her any farther than the state university, and going to school a hundred miles from home with the same crowd she knew in high school and coming home for all the holidays is really not leaving home. I think nine months away from home with a family with other children would be a valuable experience."

Shelley's parents were talking about her as if she were not present, the way they must talk about her when she heard their voices, low and earnest, after she had gone to bed.

"But California—" protested Mrs. Latham. "How would she get to San Sebastian?"

"Fly," answered Mr. Latham.

"But she would have to change planes," Mrs. Latham pointed out.

"She has to change buses when she goes downtown," said Mr. Latham.

"Please, Mother, I *want* to go," insisted Shelley. "It's only for a school year and not a whole year. And I would write every week. And it isn't as though I were going out into the world to—to seek my fortune. I'll be living with a family, a family you know, and I would be back next June. Please, Mother! Daddy, make her let me go!"

"Shelley is right," agreed Mr. Latham. "It isn't as if she were going to live with strangers."

"Yes, Mother," Shelley persisted. "And I have my school clothes all ready and all I would have to do is pack and have my records transferred and a few things like that. Say I can go. Please say I can go!"

"I seem to be overruled," said Mrs. Latham, admitting defeat with a rueful smile.

"Mother!" cried Shelley joyfully, and at the same time she was deeply touched by her mother's smile, which showed so plainly how much it hurt her mother to let her go.

"I hope this is the right decision," said Mrs. Latham, still turning the whole discussion over in her mind. "Nine whole months. If only California were not so far away—"

"Oh, Mother, everything will be all right," Shelley insisted, anxious to reassure her mother. "I know it will be all right. Everything is going to be wonderful!"

Slowly Mrs. Latham folded the tissue paper over the raincoat and replaced the lid on the box. "How much a lovely raincoat like this would have meant to me when I was sixteen," she remarked sadly. "I was sixteen during the Depression and I wanted a raincoat more than anything in the world. I had to carry a shabby old cotton umbrella to school and I was so ashamed of it."

Shelley was silent. It hurt her to see her mother look so sad. She wanted to say, But this is not the Depression and I don't want a raincoat, but she could not say it. She could not say to her mother, I am not you. I am me.

The ring of the telephone interrupted Shelley's thoughts. "It's Jack," she remarked as she picked up the receiver.

"Hi, Shelley," said the familiar voice. "Has anything exciting happened?"

"Yes!" answered Shelley, for once glad that Jack had asked that question. She was eager to tell her news to someone, to make sure it was really true. The rest, she knew, was going to be easy. All she had to do was say good-by. And in California, she was sure, she would find the boy she had always wanted to meet.

Chapter 2

As the plane began to lose altitude to land at the Vincente Municipal Airport, the landing field nearest San Sebastian, Shelley fastened her seat belt with trembling fingers. It was ridiculous for her fingers to behave that way. She was eager to begin her new life. Of course she was. It was just that everything had happened so fast and the world seen from the air was such a strange place, like a giant relief map. Cars were ants on ribbon highways and farms were old-fashioned crazy quilts. Lakes were puddles, trees on the mountains had toothpick trunks, and finally in California so much of the map was flat and brown with dust-colored hills like miniature circus tents. It did not seem real at all.

The plane landed on the runway with a gentle bounce and as it taxied toward the airport building that a moment ago had looked like a shoe box, all Shelley could think of was that now she could unpin the ten-dollar bill that her mother had insisted she pin to her slip in case she lost her purse when she changed planes. Shelley had not wanted to pin that bill to her slip—at sixteen she was certainly old enough to hang onto her purse—and she had started to protest but had thought better of it. Talking about the ten-dollar bill and what she should do if she lost her money had helped fill those last awkward minutes at the airport this morning, when she was about to leave home for the first time in her life and suddenly discovered she did not know what to say to her mother and father. And what was even more surprising, her mother and father did not seem to know what to say to her. Oh, they said the expected things like Be careful of strangers, and Study hard, and Don't forget to write, but Shelley knew that these remarks were only meant to fill up the long minutes until her plane was announced.

Shelley unfastened the seat belt and remembered how surprised she had been to learn that at sixteen there were so many things a girl could not say to her mother and father—things like I'm both glad and sorry to be leaving, and I really do feel dreadful about grinding up those roses in the Disposall, and Please don't look so sad behind your smiles—nine months isn't forever and I'll write often.

The heat, as Shelley stepped through the door of the plane, was like the blast of a hair-dryer against her face. She walked down the steps and as soon as she stepped onto the concrete, the door was shut behind her, the steps were rolled away, and the plane, her last link with everything she had known, was heading down the runway once more. I'll pretend I'm a stranger in a foreign land, Shelley told herself, and tried to feel a little braver. Somehow her legs carried her through the gate toward a woman with curly hair touched with gray whom she recognized as Mavis.

"Shelley!" cried Mavis Michie. "How wonderful to see you after all these years! We're so glad to have you!"

"I'm glad to be here," Shelley smiled shakily. "Mother sends her love."

Mavis led the way to a battered station wagon. As they left the Vincente airport and headed toward San

Sebastian, Shelley settled back for her first look at California from the ground. In that spot California was flat and brown, shimmering in the heat, and not at all what Shelley had expected, although exactly what she had expected she did not know. Something lush and tropical, perhaps.

Mavis pointed to a row of towering trees and identified them as eucalyptus. Shelley noticed that their smooth trunks were shedding their bark in long, ragged strips. She had never seen a tree shed bark before and had, in fact, been told that a tree could not live without bark. Apparently things were different in California. In the distance, against the mountains they were approaching, was a row of palm trees, the first Shelley had ever seen. They looked to her like a row of shabby feather dusters balanced on their handles. Then the station wagon rattled across a bridge and Shelley was shocked at what she saw below. *There was no water in the river bed.* Never in her whole life had Shelley seen a river without water.

Next the station wagon passed a stretch of orange trees. A grove, thought Shelley, and not an orchard. How tidy it looked. The trees were round, with branches so low they touched the ground. The green oranges looked as if they might have been hung among the leaves for decoration. Even the soil beneath the trees was arranged in neat furrows.

"What are those round metal things between the trees?" asked Shelley.

"Smudge pots," answered Mavis. "If there is danger of frost the pots, which are filled with oil, are lighted to keep the oranges from being frostbitten."

"You mean they heat up the *outdoors*?" Shelley asked incredulously.

Mavis laughed. "Enough to save the crop."

Then Shelley saw a startling billboard that an-

nounced in big red letters, "Rain for Rent." Shelley
could not believe what she read until a closer view
revealed the words, "Farm sprinkler systems for rent
or sale." The next sign that attracted her attention
was painted orange with black letters that proclaimed,
"Giant Orange 300 yards," Now I know exactly how
Alice in Wonderland felt when she fell down the
rabbit hole, thought Shelley, as she watched to see
what a Giant Orange might be. It was a roadside
stand shaped like an orange, which bore the sign,
"Fresh tree-ripened orange juice. Foot-long hot dogs."

Shelley felt reassured as they entered the town of
San Sebastian. She saw much that was familiar—a
J. C. Penney store, Shell and Standard service stations
just like those at home, a theater advertising a movie
she had seen only last week. It was the setting for the
familiar that was strange to her—the dry heat, the
palms, the orange trees and, everywhere, dusty geraniums actually growing outdoors in the ground.

After they passed through the business district, the
orange trees became more numerous and the Spanish
houses with tile roofs gave way to ranch houses. "Here
we are," said Mavis suddenly, turning into a driveway
beside a high privet hedge.

Here I am, Shelley's thought echoed, as she stepped
out of the station wagon and through the opening in
the hedge. To her surprise she found herself facing a
very old two-story clapboard house. It was painted
gray with green shutters and in the center of the front
door, which was beneath a vine covered with magenta
blossoms, was an old-fashioned doorbell such as Shelley had not seen since she had visited a great-aunt
when she was a little girl. It was a doorbell with a
handle to twirl instead of a button to push. And I
thought everything in California was modern, Shelley
marveled.

"Welcome to our house," said Mavis. "I know you want to change into something cooler. You must be dreadfully warm in a suit." She led Shelley into the house and up a flight of creaky stairs. "And here is your room. The bathroom is at the end of the hall." Mavis smiled and patted Shelley's shoulder. "It's all so strange the first time away from home, isn't it? Come on down when you have freshened up. Supper will be ready in a little while and you can meet the rest of the family then."

Grateful for a moment alone, Shelley sat down on the bed, which was covered with an India print spread, and looked around the long, narrow room. Because of the low, sloping ceiling, the sills of the windows were only a few inches from the floor. The windows looked out on a tangle of vines and treetops. Between the windows was a desk, painted black, and on the desk a pair of old flatirons, gilded and obviously intended to be used for book ends. At the end of the room between two closets was an old-fashioned dresser waiting for her lipstick and bobby pins. On the wall over the bed were two unframed Japanese prints. Opposite the windows were two doors that led into the hall (that was odd—two doors into the hall) and between them was her trunk, waiting to be unpacked. Shelley, who all her life had slept in a square room with one door, framed pictures, and windows a conventional distance from the floor, felt even more strongly that she had fallen down a rabbit hole into a new life.

Quickly she slipped out of her suit and into a cotton dress that she had brought in her overnight bag in case her trunk had not arrived. She ran a comb through her hair before she walked down the hall to the bathroom, which was like no bathroom she had ever seen before. Because of its size, she guessed that it had once been a bedroom. The windows, curtained in red-and-yellow calico, looked out upon a row of eucalyptus trees and, beyond them, an orange grove. Around the bathroom were seven towel racks, each labeled with a name printed on adhesive tape— Mavis, Tom, Katie, Luke, Shelley, Mother, Guests. Whose mother? Shelley wondered as she washed her hands and dried them on a towel from her rack. The rough white towel had the words "Santa Theresa Union High School" printed on a green stripe down the center, and as Shelley examined the bathroom more closely she saw that all the towels were white, with the name of a school printed or stitched on them. This seemed peculiar and she felt a moment of longing for the white bathroom at home with its fluffy pink towels carefully selected to match the tile. She was relieved, though, to see the names *Mavis* and *Tom*, for that was how she thought of Mr. and Mrs. Michie. Obviously they thought of themselves that way too.

Then, noticing the open lid of the hamper, Shelley closed it without thinking, because she had been brought up always to close drawers and cupboard doors. She was startled when this brought forth an indignant meow from inside the hamper. She lifted the lid and looked in at a small gray cat, the color of the shadow of a cat, blinking at her in annoyance from a heap of bath towels. "Oh—I'm sorry," apologized Shelley, and left the lid open. Obviously this family cared more for the comfort of the cat than the tidiness of the bathroom. For the first time since she stepped off the plane, Shelley's face relaxed into a smile.

Shelley was about to leave the bathroom when a commotion below led her back to the window. A tall man in a sweat shirt was bending low over the handle bars of a bicycle as he rode along the row of eucalyptus trees and disappeared around the corner of the house. He was followed by a shouting boy and girl, also on bicycles, and a large, barking police dog. They must be Tom and Katie and Luke, Shelley realized as she listened to their laughter and shouting from the other side of the house. Californians and their outdoor living!

Timidly Shelley left the bathroom and descended the stairs, hesitating a moment to look at the living room. It, too, was an unusually long, narrow room. There was a quaint old fireplace, and on its mantel an old walnut clock with a cupid painted on the glass was ticking. On either side of the fireplace bookshelves reached to the ceiling. The chairs and couches wore bright print slip covers. At the far end of the living room was a pair of doors, each topped by a glass transom. From the other side of these doors Shelley heard the rattle of dishes. The least she could do was offer to set the table, so she walked the length of the living room and tried one of the doors. It was locked.

"Come around through the dining room, Shelley," Mavis called through the door.

Shelley walked through the dining room (no one she knew at home had linoleum and painted furniture in the dining room) and into the kitchen, where she found Mavis shredding salad greens into a wooden bowl. "Shelley, would you mind doing this while I put the fake Stroganoff together?" she asked. "The rice is already cooking."

"I'd be glad to," said Shelley, wondering what fake Stroganoff could be. If things were reversed and someone had come to Shelley's home from California, her mother would have had a special dinner with fried chicken, home-made rolls and angel food cake with orange icing, all of them genuine, none of them fake.

Outside, the trio on bicycles and the barking dog tore past.

"Anything to amuse the dog," observed Mavis. "They'll all be in shortly and you can meet them."

Shelley felt a little hurt by the casualness of this family toward herself, a guest who had traveled so far. At her own home she would not have been allowed to ride around the house on a bicycle when a guest had arrived. She must remember she was a stranger in a foreign land, she told herself sternly, and she must accept the customs of the natives. They were probably right—after all, she was to be a member of the family for the winter and there was no reason why she should be treated like company.

"I'd better explain about those doors that don't open," Mavis said, as she sliced onions into melted butter in an earthenware casserole. "You see, this house was once a boardinghouse in the center of town. When it was to be torn down to make way for a filling station, Tom had a chance to buy it for practically nothing. We had it moved up here and knocked out a lot of partitions—the rooms had been very small— and that is why we have so many long, narrow rooms and why you have two doors in your bedroom. We didn't know what to do about those doors at the end of the living room, so we just left them where they were. We can't open them, because we have the refrigerator against one and some cupboards against the other."

"It—it's very nice," said Shelley, aware that "nice" was not the word she wanted to use. She did not know the exact word to describe it—shabby and comfortable and like no house she had ever seen before. No one at home lived in a converted boardinghouse. No one at home left the hamper open for the convenience of the cat.

Mavis took three packages of frozen sirloin tips out of the refrigerator, tore them open, and added their contents to the onion and butter in the casserole which she put into the oven. "There," she said. "Now all I have to do is add sour cream at the last minute."

The back door opened and the rest of the family burst into the kitchen. "Well, look who's arrived!" Tom exclaimed, and gave Shelley a hearty hug before he held her off to look at her. "Shelley, it's good to have you here!"

"Hello, Shelley," said Luke, with a smile that was shy but friendly.

"Hi," said Katie, taking in Shelley's shoes and dress and hair.

So this was the girl for whom she was to be a good experience. Uncomfortable under her scrutiny, Shelley managed to smile, uncertain what to say to three strangers at the same time. They all looked tan and healthy and there was a look of the out of doors about them. Tom and Luke she liked at once, because she felt they liked her, but Katie she was not so sure about. Perhaps this sturdy thirteen-year-old was not pleased to have another girl in the house being a good experience for her.

"Go on, all of you, and wash up for supper," ordered Mavis. "It's such a warm day we'll eat out under the pergola."

Pergola was such an old-fashioned word. Shelley had thought everyone in California had a patio.

"Katie, you slice the French bread and carry it out to the table," directed Mavis.

As she opened the breadbox, Katie heaved a noisy, exhausted sigh, as if slicing bread were a terrible chore.

"It's just a phase," said Mavis grimly.

"Mommy, do you have to go around saying everything I do is just a phase all the time?" asked Katie.

Mavis laughed. "I certainly hope it is just a phase," she said. "I would hate to think that some of your behavior was permanent."

Katie picked a leaf of curly chicory out of the salad, held it up beside her face as if it were a lock of hair, and remarked, "I wish I had curly hair."

Mavis stirred sour cream into the bubbling casserole before she ladled the Stroganoff over rice. The meal was served on trays and Shelley noticed that there was a fresh cloth napkin on each tray. She would have expected such a casual family to use paper napkins.

The Michies carried their trays out through the dining room to a table under the pergola, which Shelley saw was a sort of arbor supported by pillars and covered with vines. As she joined the family at the long table she was aware of a lovely fragrance. "Why, there are lemons growing on that tree and blossoms, too!" she exclaimed, when she had discovered the source of the fragrance. Real lemons growing in the garden!

Everyone laughed. "Haven't you ever seen lemons before?" asked Katie.

"Not growing," answered Shelley. "Why, there are green lemons and ripe lemons and blossoms on the tree all at the same time!" Nature in California must be in a state of utter confusion to produce such a tree as this.

While the others were discussing lemons, Katie left the table and walked across the yard to a tree with a gnarled trunk and slender gray foliage. She picked something, which she laid on the table in front of Shelley. "We have olives growing in the yard, too," she said.

"Fresh olives right off the tree!" marveled Shelley.

How kind of Katie to offer her one. "I simply adore olives.

"Oh, Shelley—" began Mavis.

It was too late. Shelley bit eagerly into the olive. The taste was so bitter and so terrible that she could not believe it. She sat shocked, not knowing what to do.

Katie went into a fit of giggles.

"Oh, Shelley, I am so sorry," said Mavis. "I tried to warn you."

Shelley swallowed and gulped from her water glass while Katie continued to giggle.

Then Tom spoke. "Katie, that was not a nice thing to do. I think you should apologize to Shelley."

Katie tried to look repentant but did not succeed. "I'm sorry," she said, giggling, "but you looked so surprised when you bit into the olive."

Shelley was so embarrassed she did not know how to answer. Apparently Katie had made her the victim of a practical joke. And just when she was beginning to feel at ease, too.

"All olives are bitter until they have been cured," Tom explained. "Katie was counting on your not knowing that."

"She certainly caught me," said Shelley, managing to smile to show she was a good sport, even though she did not feel like one. If this was part of Katie's difficult age, she did not like to think what the rest of the winter could be like. "It tasted so awful I don't see how anyone ever thought of eating them in the first place."

"You know, that is exactly what I have always wondered," said Katie, smiling warmly at Shelley for the first time, as if now they had something in common. "Well, I guess I had better go do my practicing."

"Mother, she's just trying to get out of the dishes," protested Luke. "She always gets out of the dishes."

"I have to practice, don't I?" asked Katie virtuously, as she rose from the table.

"Yes, you do," agreed Mavis, "but that doesn't mean you get out of the dishes."

Katie heaved a sigh that showed she was exhausted, abused, and misunderstood by her family. Then she disappeared into the house, and chords crashed out of the piano in the living room.

When Katie settled down to play, Shelley thought she played surprisingly well for a girl of thirteen. The music she recognized as Liszt's *Second Hungarian Rhapsody,* but while she listened, the rhapsody turned suddenly and logically into *Pop Goes the Weasel.*

"Katie!" yelled Tom, in a voice that would have carried across a gymnasium full of shouting boys.

The music stopped. "But Daddy," protested Katie. "It fits there. See, the music goes like this"—she demonstrated with a few notes—"and then it just naturally wants to turn into *Pop Goes the Weasel.* Like this."

"You stick to the notes as they are written," ordered Tom.

Mavis sighed. "She has talent, but she simply doesn't care."

Katie finished playing *Pop Goes the Weasel.* The rest of the family continued to sit under the pergola while darkness fell.

Shelley peered at her watch. "It is getting dark awfully early," she observed.

"That's because you are farther south. A thousand miles makes a big difference in the time darkness falls," Tom explained.

Why, I knew that, Shelley thought suddenly, but the information had never seemed real before, any more than igloos or the international date line or a lot of other things in schoolbooks seemed real. Until now this had been a fact to be learned, stored away, and pulled out again to be put down on a test paper if that question happened to be asked. Now she had really traveled, had seen before her eyes the things she had learned about in school.

Suddenly Tom rose to his feet. "There's a full moon," he announced. "Let's do the washing."

For a moment Shelley thought she must have misunderstood, but Mavis said matter-of-factly, "That's a wonderful idea. I'll gather up the laundry."

Shelley was not sure how she should react, so she offered to wash the dishes. Willing dishwashers, she knew, were always welcome. When in doubt, wash the dishes should be a good rule to follow when living in a strange household.

The Michies carried their trays into the kitchen, where Shelley began to scrape and stack the plates. From the sink she could look into the laundry, a room with a sloping roof that looked as if it had been added to the house as an afterthought. The room was equipped with an automatic washing machine, a pair of laundry tubs, an old washing machine with a wringer, two ironing boards, and a mangle so large it must have belonged to a professional laundry at one time. On the wall over the mangle was the mounted head of a deer with several old hats hung jauntily on its antlers.

While Shelley washed and wiped the dishes, Mavis sorted piles of towels, sheets, and clothing. Luke loaded the automatic washer while Tom put colored clothing through the second washing machine. They all appeared to be enjoying themselves. From the living room came the first notes of the rhapsody.

"Katie's starting that piece again just to get out of helping," remarked Luke.

Beneath her feet Shelley could feel the old house shake from the vibration of the automatic washer. A frightened mouse ran out from under a cupboard and stared at Shelley, with its whiskers quivering, before it disappeared under the refrigerator. Shelley, who had never lived in a house with mice before, did not feel surprised. A little gray mouse seemed a perfectly natural member of this household.

When Shelley had wrung out the dishcloth and hung it over the faucet, she went into the laundry. "May I help?" she asked.

"You're just in time," answered Tom, piling clean wet clothes into a clothesbasket on a child's wagon. "You and Luke can start hanging these out."

Luke pulled the wagon out into the back yard under the clotheslines. Shelley followed, thinking how strange it was to be living in the same house with a boy so near her own age and how much stranger to be hanging out laundry with him. She picked up a clothespin and began to pin a towel to the line. The moonlight, even filtered through the eucalyptus trees, was so bright that she could read the words "Vincente Junior College," printed in a green stripe down the center of the towel. The eucalyptus trees gave off a medicinal odor something like cough drops, which mingled with the sweetness of the lemon blossoms.

"I understand you are working on a motorcycle," said Shelley, wanting to start a conversation with this quiet boy.

"Yes." Luke sounded pleased at her interest. "It keeps me broke buying parts, but I think I can get it running sometime."

"Won't it worry your mother to have you riding around on a motorcycle?" Shelley asked.

"I guess so." Luke sounded discouraged, as if he had been losing an argument for a long time.

Shelley wished she had not mentioned his mother. Tom, followed by Mavis, carried out a second basket of laundry, which they began to hang. Shelley, who had a towel with "St. Joseph's High School" stitched in one corner, remarked, "You certainly have a lot of towels."

Mavis laughed. "I suppose our towels look odd to you. You see, visiting teams playing at the high school bring their own towels with them and they usually leave one or two behind. Tom started bringing them home when he discovered the janitors only threw them away. Tom never wants anything to be wasted."

"We use towels for everything—dusting, mopping up whatever gets spilled, wiping the dog's muddy feet," said Tom.

The moon, rising above the eucalyptus trees, shone even brighter. I wonder where the moon is in the sky at home, Shelley wondered, as she picked up another towel and clothespin; but no matter where it was, she was sure that no one else was hanging out a washing by its light. It seemed too bad when she thought about it. It was such a lovely way to hang out a washing. Shelley pulled the last towel out of the basket, and as she pinned it to the line she decided that if it were not for Katie, she would like living here. So far she enjoyed the customs of the natives. Tom was friendly, Mavis comfortable, Luke shy and quiet, but Katie . . . Shelley could not bring herself to like Katie wholeheartedly. And she not only had nine months of Katie's company ahead of her, but she was supposed to be a good experience for her, which probably meant to be a good example.

From inside the house came the frisking notes of *Pop Goes the Weasel.*

"Katie!" shouted Tom. *Pop Goes the Weasel* turned into the rhapsody.

Later that evening after she had unpacked her trunk and taken her turn at the towel-filled bathroom, Shelley was sitting on her bed in her pajamas, putting her hair up in pin curls. The edge of the India print spread was not even hemmed, she noticed. She was thinking that at home everything was hemmed when she heard a knock at her door.

"Come in," she said.

Katie entered. She was wearing a full red-and-white printed skirt and a white blouse with little buttons like strawberries down the front. In her hand she carried a half-eaten banana. She twirled around so that the skirt stood out. "See my dress for the first day of school!" she said, and her face shone with pleasure. "Mommy bought it for me and I wasn't even hounding her." She sank down on the bed beside Shelley and took a big bite of banana. "You know something?" she said, sounding wistful even though her mouth was full. "I wish my hair looked nice like yours."

"Why, thank you," answered Shelley, pleased by this compliment.

"Do you have a permanent?" asked Katie.

"No, my hair is curly if I coax it," replied Shelley. "It may take a lot of coaxing here, because the air is so dry."

"Do you have lots of boy friends at home?" asked Katie bluntly.

"Not lots." Katie's admiration made her feel attractive and popular, a pleasant feeling for any girl to experience.

"I wish Mommy would let me have a permanent," said Katie wistfully, running her hand through her straight dark hair. "Pamela—she's my best friend—

has permanents all the time. If I ever have a daughter my age I'll let her have all the permanents she wants."

That sounds familiar, thought Shelley with a twinge of amusement. She wondered if Katie kept a list.

"Katie!" Tom's voice rang out. "Bedtime!"

"Yes, Daddy," answered Katie in her exhausted voice. She stuffed the rest of the banana into her mouth. " 'Night, Shelley," she said, her voice muffled. "And I really am sorry about the olive. I just couldn't resist it."

"Oh, well, I guess everyone has to be a greenhorn or tenderfoot or something sometime," answered Shelley, this time forgiving Katie. When Katie had gone, she turned off the light and slipped into bed. She lay enjoying the fragrance of the lemon blossoms below her window and listening to the strange night sounds —the rustle of eucalyptus leaves, the dry rattle of palm fronds, the sound of tires on the road, the friendly creaks of an old house settling for the night, and in the distance the blat-blat of a diesel train. Where were the lonesome whistles, the a-hooey, a-hooey of song writers, Shelley wondered. Nobody wrote songs about the blat-blat of a diesel train, but then it wasn't a lonely sound.

Shelley smiled in the darkness, her uneasiness about living with a strange family now completely banished. The only thing wrong with Katie was her age. She was thirteen years old. Now that Shelley understood this, she knew that everything was going to be all right after all. She was going to like living in a house with a cat in a hamper and mice in the kitchen and a family that hung out the washing by the light of the moon.

But tomorrow was the first day of school. . . .

Chapter 3

The morning heat made Shelley languid, and feeling as if she were moving in slow motion, she walked down the creaking stairs to join the family for breakfast.

"But Mommy, Pamela's mother lets her stay up to watch the Hit Parade," Katie was saying. "I don't see why I can't."

"Good morning, Shelley!" Tom's voice would have carried across a basketball court. "You're just in time to help bring in the washing."

Shelley smiled. At home washing was hung out in the morning, not brought in.

"Go on, Katie, help Luke and Shelley," said Mavis, who was standing over a skillet of bacon while Tom supervised the toast he was making under the broiler.

"Well, I don't care," said Katie, as the three went out into the back yard. "I don't see why I never get to do the things Pamela and the other girls get to do."

"Pamela is a creep," said Luke concisely.

"She is not!" retorted Katie. "She's smooth." Katie unpinned a sheet and stuffed it into the laundry basket. "Pamela lives in a ranch house with two bathrooms."

"She's still a creep," said Luke.

Shelley enjoyed the feel of the rough clean towels

that shone so dazzlingly in the morning sun. As she folded them she looked around the yard by daylight. The house, she now discovered, was set in the middle of a large piece of property—how large she could not guess. Perhaps it was an acre. At least it was the size of eight or ten city lots at home. The yard was a pleasant tangle of trees, shrubs, and vines, most of them strange to Shelley. A double garage with a room above it—Mavis's studio, Shelley learned later, where she had her potter's wheel—stood at the back of the property and in the garage Shelley could see Luke's motorcycle. Both tires were flat, one fender was missing, and it looked so battered she wondered how he ever expected to get it to run.

At the side of the house under the eucalyptus trees that bordered the driveway was a child's slide. In front of the slide, near the end of a single rope suspended from the top of one of the trees, dangled a ring, the kind children swung on in parks. Katie dropped a sheet into the clothesbasket and walked over to the rope. She took the end of it in her hand, climbed the slide, grasped the ring, and swung out over the road with her hair and skirt flying.

"Hey, you're supposed to be helping!" yelled Luke.

"I have to wait till it stops, don't I?" answered Katie. Gradually the rope stopped swinging and Katie dropped to the ground.

"Breakfast!" called Tom.

After breakfast Tom was the first member of the family to leave for school with his lunch in a paper bag. Then Luke, with his paper bag, left earlier than was really necessary and Shelley suspected he did not want to be seen walking to school with her. It was funny how much younger a fifteen-year-old boy could be than a sixteen-year-old girl. Then Pamela appeared at the kitchen door and Shelley could see what Katie

meant about Pamela's being smooth. She was small
and trim. She made Katie, in her full red-and-white
skirt, look brown and sturdy but awkward in a nice
way, like a teddy bear in a dirndl. The two younger
girls set off in the direction of the junior high school.

It was Shelley's turn to go forth with her brown
paper bag in hand.

"Don't worry about a thing," advised Mavis with
a smile. "I'm sure you'll make a lot of friends."

Shelley did not like her feelings to show so plainly
to Mavis. "I'm not worried," she answered lightly
and untruthfully.

As Shelley walked to school she thought nervously
of new girls who had transferred to her high school
at home—the homesick girl from the South whose
honey-thick accent had so amused the class the first
day of school that the girl had looked as if she were
about to cry. And a girl who was so determined to
establish herself with the right crowd that she made
a nuisance of herself with those who were popular,
snubbed those who were not popular, and succeeded
only in making herself lonely and unhappy. And
that new girl who was so anxious to be noticed that
she took off her shoes the minute school was out and
walked barefooted to the bus, explaining that she
simply hated wearing shoes. Everyone had laughed
good-naturedly at this and the crisp autumn days
soon put an end to her pose.

Naturally I'm not going to do any of those silly
things, Shelley told herself, as she walked along the
road through the orange groves. She would be extra-
cautious about everything she said until she had made
some friends. And she would make friends. Of course
she would. Everyone had friends.

But Shelley felt less brave as she approached San
Sebastian Union High School, a tan stucco building

with a missionlike tower in the center and a row of scraggly palm trees across the front. The lawn was colorful with the gay cotton dresses of the girls, so different from the girls at home, who would be wearing their newest sweaters and skirts. Shelley was aware of the curious stares of the other students as she walked up the front steps of the school. Everyone was so tanned that Shelley felt pale—it had been a wet summer at home. There was something else different, too. The students seemed older, and then Shelley remembered that there were no freshmen here. The ninth grade attended junior high school. Among the tan faces there was not a single face that Shelley had ever seen before and yet somewhere among them were her companions for the next nine months. She made her way through the crowds of students busy renewing acquaintances after their summer vacation to the office, where she found—thank goodness!—that her records had arrived from her school at home, and where she was assigned to a registration room.

It was on her way to this room that Shelley first saw the boy. He was standing in the hall talking with a group of boys and Shelley knew at once that this was the boy she wanted to meet. She did not know why, but there was something about him that she liked at once. He was tall, with fair hair bleached by the sun, and he was deeply tanned except for a red patch on his nose where the tan had peeled off. It was not just his looks that attracted Shelley. It was something else about him. Perhaps it was the way he stood, which seemed almost graceful, or perhaps it was a sort of dignity about him. Shelley did not know. She only knew that here was a boy she wanted to meet and at the moment there was nothing she could do about it. A girl could not go up to a boy in the hall, tap him on the arm, and say, "Excuse me. I want to meet you."

Reluctantly Shelley walked away from the boy, located her registration room, and slid into the first vacant seat she saw. Chattering stopped for a moment as students glanced at the new girl. She stared at her hands, clasped on the desk in front of her. She wanted to begin to make friends but she did not know how to start.

Someone tapped Shelley on the shoulder and she found herself looking at a dark-haired boy with lively brown eyes who was sitting across the aisle.

"Don't tell me," he said as if he were cautioning her. "I have it—your last name begins with L."

"Why, yes," she admitted. "But how did you know?"

"I'm psychic," he said modestly.

"Don't let him kid you," said someone behind Shelley. "We are grouped alphabetically. This room is L's, M's, N's, and a couple of stray O's. He's just lucky he chose the right letter."

"She didn't take my hint," observed the brown-eyed boy.

"What hint?" asked Shelley.

"All right, I'll say it right out loud," answered the boy. "What's your name?"

Shelley could not help laughing at having missed something so obvious. "Shelley Latham," she replied. "I'm spending the winter with the Michies."

"You mean Slats Michie, the basketball coach?" asked the boy.

"Why, yes," answered Shelley, "only I didn't know he was called Slats."

Everyone was interested. "He's a swell guy," said a boy.

"You're sure lucky," remarked a tall girl, "living in the same house with the basketball coach."

Why, it's going to be easy, thought Shelley. All she
had to do was say she was spending the winter with
the coach's family and everyone was interested. She
wondered why she had not thought of this before.
"What's your name?" she asked the brown-eyed boy.

"Hartley Lathrop," he answered as a teacher entered the room.

The teacher read the names on the roll and asked
the students to take seats in alphabetical order. Shelley found herself sitting in front of Hartley.

"Latham, Lathrop," he whispered. "I'll always sit
behind you."

Unconsciously Shelley put her hand to the back of
her hair to make sure it was in order.

"Your hair looks fine," he whispered making Shelley
feel extremely foolish.

It seemed to Shelley that she spent the rest of the
day hunting for her classrooms and trying to make a
few faces in this building full of strangers seem familiar. Students were friendly and interested in the
new girl but Shelley could not feel that she belonged.
Even the sight of Hartley would have helped, but
he was not in any of her classes. Latin, English, physical education, lunch period. While Shelley ate her
sandwiches on the lawn, she was included in the conversation of a group of girls. She tried to remember if
she had seen any of them during the morning but she
was not sure. When their conversation turned to their
summer vacations, Shelley felt like an outsider, a
paleface among the natives.

After lunch period came that part of the day set
aside for activities. The morning bulletin had said
that class meetings would be held at this time, so
Shelley made her way alone to the study hall on the
second floor, where her class, the Low Elevens, was
meeting. Even being a member of the Low Elevens

seemed odd. At home she would have been called a Fifth-termer. Shelley slipped into a seat near the door. At home she would have known everyone in her class and would not have this left-out feeling. At home Jack would probably be sitting beside her. What was she thinking about anyway? She didn't want Jack to sit beside her. She wanted to be in San Sebastian, didn't she? All right then. All she needed was a little time.

And then Shelley saw the face that she knew she would not forget. It was the face of the boy she had seen in the hall that morning. Now he was leaning against the window sill, talking to two other boys. She wondered if the three of them might be on the basketball team, because they were all tall and athletic-looking. A girl spoke to him and the boy flashed her a shy, lopsided grin that made Shelley skip a breath, even though the grin was not meant for her.

"Will the meeting please come to order?" It was Hartley Lathrop who spoke from the front of the room.

Shelley forced herself not to stare at the tall boy by the window.

"We will dispense with the reading of the minutes," announced Hartley, "because this is our first meeting and we don't have any." This brought loud applause from the boys in the class.

"Our first problem is to raise some money for our class fund," Hartley went on, "and since we have always done it by selling something on the front lawn at noon and since we have permission from the office to sell something a week from Monday, does anyone have any suggestions as to what we should sell?"

"I nominate Sno-cones," someone called out.

"No! No!" protested several voices all at once. "Everybody sells Sno-cones."

"Order!" shouted Hartley. "Sno-cones have been

nominated and if everyone will please be quiet we will have some more nominations and then take a vote."

"Dixie cups!" someone called from the back of the room.

Shelley glanced at the boy by the window. She could not take much interest in the class meeting, because she felt like an observer instead of a participant. At home all the classes would have raised money at the annual Spring Festival in the park next to the school. First there would be the crowning of the queen. Every year Shelley's mother remarked, "Shelley, wouldn't it be fun if you were chosen queen of the Spring Festival when you are a senior? You are just as pretty as any of the girls." And every year her mother was puzzled when Shelley answered, "It takes more than being pretty and anyway, I don't want to be Festival queen." After the queen was crowned, the girls' gym classes would wind the Maypole. It would be a lovely spring day—unless it rained and the whole thing was moved into the gymnasium. Each class and club would have a booth and there would be nail-driving booths and candied-apple booth and phonograph-record-breaking booths, and all the kids from the elementary school would come running when their school was out and feel grown-up to be mingling with high-school students. Shelley remembered one time when she was working in a booth. . . .

Suddenly, almost without thinking, Shelley stood up to make a nomination.

Hartley recognized her and grinned. "Miss Shelley Latham wishes to speak."

Everyone—even the boy by the window—knew her name now. Shelley moistened her lips and spoke. "I nominate doughnut holes."

For a fraction of a second the room was silent and

Shelley had a panicky feeling that she had made some terrible mistake. Then the room was filled with a shout of laughter. Shelley felt her face turn crimson as she stood there, too paralyzed by surprise to sit down. They were laughing at her. These horrible Low Elevens, as they called themselves, were laughing at her. The whole horrible roomful. She hated them! Every single one of them. Out of the corner of her eye she caught a glimpse of the boy by the window looking at her and laughing with the rest of the class. The boy she wanted to meet.

"Order! Order!" shouted Hartley, and when the room finally quieted down, he said, "Thanks for the joke, Shelley. Any more nominations?"

"But I'm not being funny," Shelley cried out in dismay. "I meant it."

The president of the Low Elevens looked puzzled. "How can we sell something that doesn't exist?" he asked.

"But they do exist," protested Shelley, and all at once the whole situation was clear to her. The students of San Sebastian High did not know about doughnut holes. Maybe the town was too small to have a doughnut shop. Of course. Why, they must have thought she was talking like a character out of *Alice in Wonderland*.

Shelley had to raise her voice to speak above the babble in the room. "I don't mean the actual hole in the doughnut," she explained. "I mean the dough that is cut out of the doughnut to make the hole. At home the doughnut shop cooked them along with the doughnuts."

"You mean we could really buy doughnut holes?" asked Hartley.

"Yes," answered Shelley. "We sold them at the

school I came from. Two for a nickel, and they were very popular."

"Doughnut holes have been nominated!" announced Hartley.

"I move the nominations be closed!" shouted half-a-dozen students.

"I second it!" everyone seemed to say at once.

Doughnut holes were chosen unanimously and one of the girls volunteered to make all the arrangements with a doughnut shop in Vincente. Shelley felt the crimson of her embarrassment turn to a flush of pleasure as everyone smiled at her, the new girl with the good idea. Now she belonged.

When the bell rang and the meeting was adjourned, Hartley sought out Shelley, who was finding it very pleasant to feel like a member of the class. "Thanks for the swell idea," he said. "I didn't know there were any new ideas for selling things left. Where are you headed for?"

Shelley consulted her schedule. "Biology lab. Room 211. I guess everyone thought I was crazy at first, but I thought every town had a doughnut shop."

Hartley grinned at her. "What we needed was some new blood around here."

"That's me," answered Shelley. "A regular transfusion."

"Maybe you and I should drive down to Vincente sometime to sample the doughnut holes," said Hartley.

"Maybe," answered Shelley, smiling. He had said maybe and she did not want to be any more definite than he. Even so, she felt heady with success. She had walked right into a new school and had made herself a part of the class the very first day. And now the president of the class was walking down the hall with her and she almost had a date with him.

"Here's where I'm going. Chemistry. Right next door to biology," said Hartley.

" 'By," said Shelley with a smile. Hartley had not really made a date but she was not worried. Latham, Lathrop. She would see him often. If only he were the tall boy with the sunburned nose. . . .

Shelley entered the biology laboratory, a room that was so hot she felt stifled. The study of a laboratory science, one of the requirements for college entrance, was to be a new experience for her. She sat down at one of four vacant chairs at a table which was covered with a film of dust that had been partially erased by the arms and notebooks of a previous class. The room was on the west side of the building and the shades were drawn almost to the sills to keep out the afternoon sun.

A girl, tiny and as alert-looking as a sparrow, sat in the chair opposite Shelley. "Hello," she said with a friendly smile. "That was a wonderful idea you had about doughnut holes." Then before Shelley could answer she called to someone behind Shelley, "Hi, Phil! Here's a chair."

Shelley turned and saw two boys. One was tall and heavy and one of the healthiest-looking boys Shelley had ever seen. He looked as if he ate steak three times a day. The other was the boy with the sunburned nose.

"Hi, Jeannie," they both said. The heavy boy sat in the chair beside Jeannie and the other boy sat beside Shelley. From the look of disappointment on Jeannie's face, Shelley knew that this boy must be Philip.

Shelley smiled at Philip, who glanced down at the table top for an instant before he flashed her the shy, lopsided grin that made Shelley skip a breath for the second time that day. He was perfect, she decided instantly, and glanced away, realizing that Jeannie's sharp eyes had missed neither her smile nor Philip's grin. Philip. Shelley was intensely aware of him even though she dared not look at him.

A man stepped behind a counter at the front of the room and addressed the class. "If you will do me the honor of giving me your attention—"

Oh, dear, a man teacher, thought Shelley. They were always harder than women teachers, especially when they were the sarcastic type.

"I will pass around this diagram of the tables. Sign your names in the appropriate spaces," continued the teacher, whose name was Mr. Ericson.

Why, that means we will have these seats for the whole semester, thought Shelley. She would sit beside Philip for a whole term. What luck. What glorious luck! She glanced quickly at Philip, hoping that Jeannie would not notice. What a nice-looking boy he was. And that sunburned patch on his nose—there was something so— so touching about it.

Shelley forced her attention back to her teacher, who was saying, "Biology is, as I hope you already know, the science of living things. . . ."

Of course I know, thought Shelley, drowsy in the heat. Her thoughts drifted. Dear Mother and Daddy, she mentally wrote. Today was the first day of school. I liked all of my teachers except my biology teacher and I am not sure about him. The nicest boy named Philip sits next to me in biology. He is very good-looking. . . .

Shelley wondered what Philip's last name was and where he lived. And wouldn't it be wonderful if he really was on the basketball team and she got to wear his letter man's sweater (did boys let girls wear their sweaters down here the way they did at home?) and everybody thought how lucky she was. Dear Rosemary, Shelley began another mental letter. Today I met the most wonderful boy. He sits next to me in biology lab and he has the nicest grin. You would be simply mad about him. . . .

Shelley came out of her daydream long enough to sign the seat chart and to learn from it that the other girl at the table was Jeanne Jones, the boy who looked as if he lived on steak was Frisbie Gerard, and Philip's last name was Blanton. Philip Blanton. And he was going to sit beside her for an eighty-minute period for a whole semester. If only the room were not so oppressively warm. . . .

Shelley propped her chin on her fist and stared dreamily out the window, below the partially drawn shade, at the top of a palm tree. An honest-to-goodness palm tree in San Sebastian, California. Why, the closest she had ever been to a palm tree was in church on Palm Sunday when she had been given a bit of dried palm leaf. This was a real live palm tree. Shelley knew it was real, but she had difficulty making it seem real because here nothing seemed very real. It was all so unreal and so perfect—living on North Mirage Avenue, the wonderful Michies who hung out the washing by the light of the moon, the enthusiasm of her class at her suggestion of a dough-nut-hole sale, Philip beside her in biology lab for a whole semester. Philip, who was the kind of boy every girl dreamed of meeting. It was all like a happy dream and this was going to be a wonderful year, she knew. Her world was full of sunshine and friendly people and nothing could possibly happen to spoil it. Shelley was sure of that.

Chapter 4

Drowsy in the new climate, Shelley felt as if she were drifting through her first week in San Sebastian in a beautiful dream of sunny days, blue skies, and strange faces—faces that grew less strange as each day passed. It was a happy week. Everyone was friendly and with the exception of the sarcastic Mr. Ericson, Shelley liked her teachers. She found it pleasant to study at the black desk with the gilded flatirons for book ends and to know that Luke and Katie were studying at the dining-room table downstairs. Luke asked her help with his Latin and Shelley enjoyed helping him find the main verb in sentences similar to those she had translated the year before. Katie would drop into her room to tell her about her struggles with a book report. ("The teacher says we have to tell something about the author and I don't know anything about the author. Do you think it would be all right if I just made something up?")

And then there were letters from home. "Shelley dear," wrote her mother. "The house has seemed so quiet since you left. Every time the telephone rings I expect it to be a call for you. We miss you but are so happy you are enjoying . . ." "Dear Shell," wrote Rosemary. "Having fun lolling about under the palm trees? Guess what? Jack walked home from school with me today, not that I think you'd care. I'm just reporting the facts, ma'am. Anyway, he talked mostly about you. . . ." "Dear Shelley," wrote Jack. "Holy cow! School doesn't seem the same with you way off down there." Shelley giggled. Holy cow! Poor Jack. It seemed as if she had known him a long, long time ago.

However, there was one thing about her first week of school that bothered Shelley. That was Philip. He always greeted her with his shy grin and although he sat beside her for the eighty minutes of biology laboratory, he did not offer to start a conversation. Shelley purposely left her notebook in her locker so that she could ask to borrow paper from him. This would give her two opportunities to talk to Philip because, of course, she would have to return the paper. He loaned her the paper but somehow this did not lead to the conversation she had planned. Instead, Philip talked across the table to Frisbie while Jeannie's smile showed she had missed nothing.

"Say, Friz," Philip said before class, toward the end of the week. "Do you think we can get that topsoil moved on Saturday?"

"Sure," answered Frisbie. "If we start early enough."

"What do you mean, move topsoil?" asked Shelley. After all, sitting there at the same table she couldn't help overhearing the conversation, could she? And it didn't hurt to be friendly, did it?

"One of our neighbors who is going to put in a back lawn had a load of topsoil dumped on his driveway and Phil and I are going to move it for him," answered Frisbie. "We have formed a company. Blanton and Gerard, Contractors If the Job Isn't Too Hard. You know, pick-and-shovel work, tree cutting, wood splitting. Things that take brawn but not brains."

Shelley laughed. "Where is the topsoil you are going to move?" she asked Philip directly.

"Up the street a few blocks," he answered pleasantly, and opened his textbook.

Jeannie smiled wickedly across the table at Shelley.

Darn him, anyway, thought Shelley. What was the matter with him, acting like a yup-and-nope character in a western. She did not think he was unfriendly. He was only shy, and it was going to be up to her to find a way to make him less shy.

Mr. Ericson called the class to order and Shelley languidly opened her book. It must be difficult for a boy to be as shy as Philip. He probably felt uncomfortable around girls. Well, she would go right on being friendly toward him and maybe he would stop her in the hall sometime when Jeannie and Frisbie weren't around to hear what he said. He would look down at her with that shy grin of his and turn red and look embarrassed and say, "Shelley, I— I wondered if you were doing anything Saturday night." And she would smile to put him at his ease and say gently, "Why, no, Philip, I'm not. . . ."

"When Shelley Latham decides to join the class," said Mr. Ericson, "we shall begin."

The class laughed and Shelley felt herself blushing. If only she were not stuck with this man for a biology teacher when everything else in San Sebastian was so pleasant. Oh, well. . . . The lab was so hot in the afternoon sun. It was so hard to concentrate. Shelley's mind drifted again, this time to all the cool things she could think of—maidenhair fern growing along the streams in the woods, trilliums blooming through the last crusts of melting snow in the mountains, dark caves hollowed in the cliffs at the bottom of a waterfall where she had stood and watched the rainbows in the thundering curtain of water between her and the sunshine. Cold, cold water. . . .

That evening Shelley was introduced to another Michie custom. Because Mavis bought groceries for the whole week on Friday, supper on Thursday was always made up of the accumulation of leftovers—the one helping of beef Stroganoff, the last of the spaghetti, the one tomato, the heel of the roast. Mavis also served a platter of scrambled eggs "to fill in the cracks."

Halfway through the meal Shelley turned to Tom and asked, "Is there a boy on the basketball team named Philip Blanton?"

"Well, Shelley," answered Tom with a quizzical smile. "You, too?"

"I'll say he's on the basketball team," said Luke enthusiastically. "Last year he was just about the best forward in the whole county, is all. And he was only a sophomore."

"And all the girls are mad about him," added Katie with equal enthusiasm, "but he never bothers with any of them."

"I just wondered," said Shelley hastily, helping herself to three tablespoons of creamed tuna fish that had been served in a custard cup. "He sits next to me in biology and he is so tall I thought he must be on the basketball team."

"He is, Shelley. He is," said Tom.

"You're sure lucky to get to sit next to him," said Katie. "Do you think he'll ask you for a date?"

"Oh, Katie, don't be silly," said Shelley with a forced laugh. Katie was always so blunt.

"It would be just wonderful if he would," said Katie wistfully.

He won't," said Luke flatly. "He isn't going to waste his time on girls."

Oh, is that so, thought Shelley, even though she was afraid Luke might be right. Philip was not like a lot of athletes, the chesty kind who lounged around on the front steps at school and gave the girls they bothered to speak to that you-lucky-girl look, as if the girl should feel honored to be noticed by someone with a block letter on his sweater. Philip was pleasant and courteous to everyone, but in a reserved way. It wouldn't hurt to encourage a boy who was shy, would it?

"Katie dear, clear the table," said Mavis. Katie sighed wearily while Mavis said, "For dessert we have leftover devil's food cake, macaroons, one serving of vanilla ice cream, two servings of chocolate ice cream, and frozen pineapple. I have to get rid of it so I can defrost tonight."

"Did Katie bake the cake?" asked Luke.

"Yes, I did," said Katie, lifting a plate as if it were very, very heavy.

"Did you bake it from mix or from scratch?" Luke wanted to know.

"From cake mix," said Katie. "It won't poison you. Besides, lots of boys would be glad to have a sister who baked cake."

Shelley nibbled at a macaroon and wondered how she could help Philip overcome his shyness as far as she was concerned.

Shelley was glad when Friday afternoon arrived. The days were so warm she found it increasingly difficult to stay awake in class, particularly in the biology laboratory. It was so hard to be alert when all she wanted to do was put her head down on the table and take a nap. When it came time to go to the office of the school paper to pick up her copy of the *Bastion*, she was tempted not to bother. had to force herself to take the extra steps and when she presented her student-body card, she accepted the paper without much interest. As she walked toward her locker she glanced at the paper and saw that it contained the usual articles found in the first issue of a school paper—a welcome from the principal, a welcome from the student-body president, a picture of the captain of the football team, an editorial about not throwing lunch sacks on the lawn.

Then halfway down a column called "The Roving Reporter" a name leaped out at Shelley. Her drowsiness disappeared as she read with wide-awake interest. "Looking forward to next winter's basketball season is Phil Blanton, San Sebastian's right forward. Draping his six-foot frame over a garbage can by the gym, Phil revealed that he believes San Sebastian stands a good chance of trouncing Vincente when basketball season rolls around. In the meantime he expects to keep busy with the firm of Blanton and Gerard, Contractors If the Job Isn't Too Hard. When your reporter queried Phil about his interest in girls, he answered, 'Girls? Never heard of them.' However, his partner, Friz Gerard, who was draped over the next garbage can, was heard to comment, 'Except when they come from up North and take biology.'"

Why, that's me. Shelley quickly reread the paragraph. "'Except when they come from up North and take biology.'" The words could mean only one thing —Frisbie knew that Philip liked her. And since Frisbie was Philip's best friend and business partner, who could know him better? There it was in black and white for the whole school to see. Philip liked her.

Blessings on thee, Frisbie Gerard, thought Shelley, and her footsteps were light as she walked out of the building and through the orange groves. When she reached her room she lay down on her India print spread (at home she would have been expected to turn the spread back) and held the paper up over her head to read the words of the Roving Reporter a third time. And a fourth. Surely these were the most interesting words ever printed and surely they would give Philip the push he needed.

It occurred to Shelley that this was the first Friday night in a long time that she did not have the prospect of a date for the week end. At home she would have seen Jack whether she wanted to or not. Now she felt pleasantly carefree. Jack was over a thousand miles away, she had no date, and anything might happen. Maybe when Philip read the interview in the paper he would get up his courage to telephone. Maybe this very evening.

Later, when supper was over and Shelley and Luke had washed the dishes while Katie fed Sarge, the dog, and Smoky, the cat, Mavis remarked, "I don't know where this week has gone. I sprinkled the clothes but I haven't had a minute to do any ironing."

"Let's do it now," said Tom promptly. "Come on, everybody, we're going to iron."

Amused, Shelley followed the family into the laundry, where Tom lit the gas that heated the old-fashioned mangle and Mavis prepared to iron at the ironing board.

"Shelley, you take the other ironing board," directed Tom. "Katie, you and Luke feed the flat things into the mangle while I run it."

Obediently Shelley plugged in the iron and selected a sport shirt while Mavis started to iron one of Katie's blouses. Tom operated the lever that raised the top of the mangle. "Now!" he ordered, and simultaneously he and his two children fed napkins into the mangle.

This was the secret of the fresh napkins at each meal. Tom brought the top down on the heated cylinder and the napkins rolled in and came out ironed. They ran the napkins through to fold them, laid them aside, and reached for more unironed linen. "Now!" Tom ordered, and the operation was repeated.

Why, ironing is fun, marveled Shelley, running her iron in and out around the buttons on the sport shirt and feeling a little like a child who has finally been asked to the party. Once the telephone rang, and Shelley started. At home Friday-night calls were almost always for her. This one was not. She finished ironing the shirt and hung it from the top of the door on a hanger. As she turned back to the ironing board she noticed the head of the six-point buck. "Is that the deer's head Mother says you took to college with you?" she asked Mavis.

"Yes, it is," answered Mavis, and laughed. "Your poor mother. I'm afraid I was a terrible trial to her."

"Why?" asked Shelley, finding it difficult to imagine Mavis a trial to anyone.

"I was so untidy and our room in the dormitory was so small," explained Mavis. "I used to hang my one hat and my scarves on the antlers, because they were so handy, and every week your mother would take them down just before room inspection. She was so fastidious—she always looked as if she had just stepped out of a shower into freshly ironed clothes."

Shelley smiled, thinking that her mother still looked that way. Maybe that was why she had not wanted Shelley to wear a dirty slicker. She wanted Shelley to look the way she had looked when she was a girl. The words that Shelley had not spoken the day she threw the roses into the Disposall came back to her now. But Mother, I am not you. I am me.

"But Mommy, why did you take a deer's head away to school?" asked Katie, from the mangle.

Mavis laughed. "Why does a girl that age do anything? A boy I thought was perfectly wonderful shot the deer and had the head mounted for me, and naturally I couldn't bear to leave such a precious gift at home."

"And you've kept it all these years?" exclaimed Shelley, and realized at once that her reference to all these years was scarcely tactful.

Mavis burst out laughing. "It isn't easy to get rid of the mounted head of a six-point buck."

"Were you madly in love?" asked Katie.

"Girls in their teens always fancy themselves in love with the wrong boy," said Mavis, smiling. "However, this boy came to visit me at school, took one look at Shelley's mother, and lost interest in me."

"He did?" Shelley was amazed at this glimpse of her mother's girlhood. "But didn't you mind?"

"A little at first," admitted Mavis, "but I think I was really relieved to get rid of him, because he wanted me to hunt jack rabbits with him. Anyway, he helped make up for your mother's disappointment that week end."

"What sort of disappointment?" asked Shelley curiously.

"She didn't get elected Soph Doll," said Mavis. "That is what we called the queen of the sophomore ball."

"Soph Doll!" repeated Shelley in astonishment. *Mother* wanted to be Soph Doll?

"Yes, and it was a shame she didn't win," said Mavis. "She was the prettiest of the candidates but lost out through some sort of campus politics."

Shelley was incredulous. Mother wanting to be elected Soph Doll of all things. Of course, she was pretty for an older woman, but she was—well, a house-wife. She had been ever since Shelley had known her. Before that she had been a teacher and before that—apparently she had been a girl who hoped to be Soph Doll. For Shelley this was an entirely new picture of her mother and as she ironed another sport shirt she found herself feeling sorry that her mother had not been elected to rule over a sophomore ball a long time ago.

"And you know," Mavis continued, "I've always felt I should have turned the deer's head over to your mother along with the boy. The Great White Hunter, we called him."

In the front of the house the doorbell twirled. "You get it, Katie," directed Tom, opening the mangle once more.

Katie returned in a moment, her eyes sparkling. "Someone to see you, Shelley," she announced.

"Me?" asked Shelley, as excitement shot through her. Philip! The story in the paper had given him the push he needed.

It was Hartley Lathrop who entered the laundry behind Katie. "Hi, Shelley," said Hartley. "Good evening, Mrs. Michie and Mr. Michie."

"Why, Hartley!" In her surprise Shelley set the iron down flat.

"I know you weren't expecting me," apologized Hartley, "but at the last minute I got the car. When I tried to phone, the line was busy so I thought I'd take a chance. You can throw me out if you want to."

"Why—" Shelley was not sure what to say. She only hoped that her disappointment did not show. A scorched smell rose from her ironing board and she hastily lifted the iron.

"Not a chance," said Tom. "We're starting sheets and can use another hand around here."

"Sure," said Hartley, pulling a sheet out of the laundry basket. He and Luke folded it in half the long way while Tom and Katie folded a second sheet. They laid the ends on the roller. "Now!" said Tom. The mangle closed and the sheets rolled through.

Shelley wondered what Hartley would think. She could not picture any of the boys she knew at home helping with the ironing, any more than she could picture her mother or father asking them to help. Hartley seemed to be enjoying himself so Shelley went on with her task.

"I promised Shelley a trip to Vincente to sample doughnut holes," Hartley explained, as he picked up another sheet.

"You two run along," said Mavis. "The rest of us can finish."

"No hurry," said Hartley, folding the sheet. When the last sheet and shirt and dirndl had been ironed, he turned to Shelley. "Shall we go?" he asked.

"Yes." Shelley felt a little shy under the interested scrutiny of Katie.

"Thanks for the help, Hartley," said Tom.

"And do come over sometime when we aren't ironing," said Mavis. "We won't always put Shelley's guests to work."

Shelley enjoyed the drive through the warm evening. The stars seemed lower than the stars at home. Once there was a hint of moisture in the air as they passed a grove that had been irrigated that day. As they turned a corner the headlights caught for an instant a graceful tree with foliage that trailed in the breeze. "What was that feathery tree?" she asked.

"A pepper tree," answered Hartley.

"Oh, of course. The tree with pink berries," said Shelley. "Mavis sent us some at Christmas once when

I was in grade school and I took some to school to show the class. I felt so important."

Vincente looked very much like San Sebastian, though a little larger perhaps, and farther from the mountains. The doughnut shop, which was near the Orange Belt College, was filled with students who had stopped in on their way from the library. They made Shelley feel young and inexperienced, but Hartley was at ease. He guided her past a rack displaying every kind of doughnut—plain, sugar-coated, chocolate-frosted, nut-covered—into a booth, where he ordered doughnut holes and milk shakes. Then he smiled across the table at Shelley, who was enjoying the cinnamon and nutmeg fragrance of the shop. "Your hair looks nice in front, too," he said.

Shelley laughed and to change the subject said, "I hope you didn't mind helping with the ironing tonight."

"Not a bit. It was fun," answered Hartley. "The Michies made me feel like part of the family."

"I know," said Shelley. "They made me feel that way the minute I arrived. I was so scared. I had never been away from home before except for two weeks at camp once."

"Do you like California, Shelley?" Hartley asked seriously.

"I do now," said Shelley. "At first everything looked so flat and dry and there wasn't any water in the river bed. A river with no water—I had never seen anything like that before."

"Don't worry," said Hartley. "There will be water this winter."

"It seems hard to believe," said Shelley. "At first all I could think was that I had to spend the winter in this place. I had heard so much about California I guess I expected to step across the border into the tropics." Shelley munched a doughnut hole thought-fully before she said, "And you know, now that I'm used to it, it really is beautiful. I love it. Oranges and olives really growing on trees, and down the street from our house there is a tree with pomegranates growing on it. Real pomegranates!"

"You make them sound like something special," said Hartley. "I've seen pomegranates around here ever since we came to California when I was about three years old, and I never thought much about them."

"They remind me of a story I used to read when I was a little girl," said Shelley, thinking that Hartley had a nice face. Not as nice as Philip's, with his sunburned nose, but nice in a different way. Thinner, more sensitive, the kind of face that in the movies belonged to the man who didn't get the girl but you sort of wished he had.

"What was the story?" asked Hartley.

"I used to like fairy tales," said Shelley, "and this was a myth about Persephone, who was snatched away by Pluto to the lower world, and while she was there she ate six pomegranate seeds and that is why we have six months of summer and six months of winter."

Hartley looked at her so steadily that Shelley was embarrassed. How silly to be sitting here talking about fairy tales. She did not know what had come over her. She would never have thought of telling Jack such a thing. They were both silent a moment, and out of habit Shelley opened her mouth to say something. Then she closed it and was silent.

"You started to say something," Hartley reminded her.

Shelley looked down at the table. "Not really."

"Yes, you did," Hartley insisted.

Shelley laughed nervously. "I don't really know

what I was going to say. Just anything, I guess. A boy I—I used to know always said, 'Penny for your thoughts' when there was a silence and I guess I fell into the habit of saying anything that popped into my mind to keep him from saying it."

"Didn't you like the boy?" Hartley asked curiously.

For the first time since she had left home, Shelley stopped to think about Jack. She found that being a thousand miles away gave her a new perspective. "Yes," she said thoughtfully, "I liked him. He was really an awfully nice fellow, but you know how it is. You go out with a boy three or four times and everybody assumes you are going steady. I guess we just ran out of things to talk about." As she spoke Shelley knew that although she was tired of Jack, she was also grateful to him. He had taken her to school dances and the movies and different places to eat so that she had learned how a girl should act and could sit here with Hartley without worrying about her behavior.

Shelley stirred her milk shake with her straw. She had not meant to confide in Hartley but, for a boy, she found him surprisingly easy to talk to. And the thought crossed her mind that if he had been Philip she would have been more cautious in expressing disapproval of going steady. It was funny how a girl would behave one way with one boy and an entirely different way with another boy.

Feeling that she had let the conversation become too personal, Shelley said, "I like school, too, and next semester I get to take journalism. I've wanted to take journalism ever since I entered high school."

"I'm going to take it too," said Hartley. "I want to go to Stanford and it would help the family a lot if I could get a scholarship. And to get a scholarship you have to take part in activities. I figured that if I worked on the school paper I would get credit for an activity and an English course at the same time."

"That's a good idea," said Shelley, admiring Hartley's ability to plan ahead. They sat in silence, each thinking about individual plans for the future.

"I think doughnut holes taste better than doughnuts," said Hartley. "Maybe it is because they were your idea."

Shelley wrinkled her nose at Hartley. "I think we had better go," she said, glancing at her watch. "I'm not sure what time the Michies expect me to be in." And the funny part of it was that since no one had mentioned when she should come home, she was anxious to return early.

They said little on the way home. Hartley parked the car outside the privet hedge and walked Shelley to the door, which she found was unlocked. She opened it and Hartley stepped into the front hall with her. A lamp was shining in the living room, but Shelley was not sure whether she should ask Hartley to sit down or not.

"I won't stay," Hartley said, as if in answer to her thoughts.

"I had a good time." Shelley meant it, even though she would have preferred spending the evening with Philip.

"I like you, Shelley," said Hartley directly. "You make me feel as if I were seeing things around me for the first time. Like pepper trees. And that pomegranate tree. I've seen it all my life and never thought anything about it except when I was a kid and we used to snitch pomegranates at Halloween. But you make it seem as if having a pomegranate tree growing down the street is something special."

Shelley smiled, not knowing quite how to answer.

A girl always enjoyed hearing a boy say he liked her. Before she could think of an answer, she began to have an uneasy feeling that she and Hartley were being watched. She glanced up over Hartley's shoulder, and there in the transom over the unused door at the end of the living room was the face of Katie, beaming down at her like a Cheshire cat.

Why, she must be crouched on top of the refrigerator, thought Shelley in astonishment, and at the same time she noticed that the transom had been opened.

"Uh . . ." said Shelley, ill at ease under the interested eye of Katie. "Well, uh . . . thank you, Hartley. I had a good time."

"Shelley, I . . ." Hartley began.

"Good night, Hartley," said Shelley firmly and with what she knew was false brightness. Darn Katie anyway. Little snoop.

"Good night, Shelley," said Hartley, looking puzzled and a little hurt.

"See you at school," said Shelley, realizing that the pleasant evening was ending on an awkward note. "You know, Latham, Lathrop."

"We can't miss, can we?" answered Hartley. "Good night, Shelley."

Even if Hartley was not Philip, Shelley did not want him to go away with his feelings hurt. She glanced at the transom and saw that Katie was still watching with avid interest. She could not think of a thing to say so she said, "Good night, Hartley."

As Shelley closed the door she heard the thump of Katie jumping to the floor. Wait till I get hold of her, thought Shelley. Just wait. If Katie thought she was going to let her get away with spying on her just so she could tease . . .

Shelley did not have to wait. Katie appeared in

the living room in her pajamas. "Shelley, he said he *liked* you!" she exclaimed. "Aren't you simply thrilled to *pieces?*"

"Why, yes, I am pleased," Shelley admitted cautiously. Katie's reaction was not at all what she expected.

Katie looked at Shelley with admiration shining from her face. "It must be wonderful to have a boy say he likes you!"

Shelley did not have the heart to scold.

"I know I shouldn't have watched," said Katie, with disarming frankness, "but I just had to so if a boy ever asks me to go out I will know what to do." She paused and sighed gustily. "But I don't suppose a boy ever will ask me."

"Oh, I wouldn't say that," said Shelley, wondering if Katie would crouch on the refrigerator if Philip ever brought her home.

"What would you have done if he had tried to kiss you?" Katie asked bluntly.

Shelley made a face at Katie and put her hand on the banister rail. "I don't know—he didn't try," she said, and ran up the stairs.

Chapter 5

The next week, at school, Hartley was still friendly toward Shelley but there was a restraint in his behavior that was new. Shelley was sorry, but she did not know how to tell him about Katie's watching them say good night. A girl on top of the refrigerator was such an improbable thing to try to explain. Everything about Shelley's new life was so fresh and so exciting that she did not let her thoughts linger on anything or anybody—except Philip—very long.

Every day she found something new to like about San Sebastian Union High School. It seemed so much more friendly than the school she had attended at home and, because it was smaller, everyone knew everyone else. Shelley and Jeannie soon became friends. Jeannie was different from any girl Shelley had ever known. She was so small and quick and eager and yet beneath her eagerness she seemed wistful, as if she were waiting for something to happen and was afraid it might not.

The girls usually ate their lunches together on the lawn under a palm tree. "I think it is fun to bring a lunch when everyone does," confided Shelley one day. "It makes every lunch period seem like a picnic."

"I would like to go to a school that had a cafeteria," said Jeannie. "If all the tuna-fish sandwiches I have eaten since kindergarten were laid end to gave her an idea. "Specifically, I like basketball players who take biology," she answered with unaccustomed daring.

"Basketball players, biology," muttered the reporter, and flashed a grin at Shelley. "Thanks a lot. That should fill up my space."

"You're welcome," answered Shelley with a smile, and turned to her locker. Had she done the right thing? she wondered. Maybe Philip wouldn't like a girl who practically threw herself at him in the school paper. Maybe he would be embarrassed. But what was a girl supposed to do when a boy was shy? She had to do something and there was a chance this might work.

"Hi, Shelley," said Hartley unexpectedly. "You look as if you thought something exciting was about to happen."

"In San Sebastian, who knows?" said Shelley. Hartley grinned and walked on down the hall, and Shelley watched until he turned the corner. Sometime she must find a way to explain about Katie on the refrigerator. . . .

Half hoping the reporter would not use her statement, Shelley nervously awaited the next issue of the *Bastion*. When she received her copy she turned with trembling hands to the Roving Reporter column. There it was, her name in print. Her eye skimmed through the paragraph. She was almost afraid to look at the last sentence. " 'I like basketball players who take biology,' confessed this pert L-11 miss."

Her remark had been printed and there was nothing she could do about it now. Seeing the words in black and white made Shelley regret her statement to the reporter. She had been too bold, she was sure. And what would Tom and Mavis think when they read the paper? And what if Mavis happened to men-

tion the story when she wrote to Shelley's mother—
or even send her the clipping? Well, anyway, Shelley
told herself ruefully, it had seemed like a good idea
at the time.

When the next biology period arrived, Shelley
dreaded facing Philip. She lingered at her locker as
long as she dared, hoping that if she entered the room
just as the class started she could avoid talking to
Philip a little longer. Unfortunately Shelley under-
estimated the time it would take her to reach the
laboratory.

Mr. Ericson had already begun to talk when she
entered the room. He was silent as he looked directly
at Shelley, who was trying to slip inconspicuously into
her chair. Then he said to the class, "May I introduce
the late Shelley Latham?"

Shelley's face was crimson and she did not move
her eyes from the initials inked on the cover of the
notebook she had laid on the table in front of her.
The late Shelley Latham! Why did Mr. Ericson have
to be so sarcastic all the time anyway? She was so
annoyed with her teacher that for once she did not
feel drowsy in the afternoon heat.

"Hi, Webfoot," whispered Philip, under cover of
the laughter of the class.

Shelley did not dare look at Philip. She could not
risk any more of Mr. Ericson's sarcasm. The next
seventy-nine minutes of laboratory were difficult for
Shelley. She tried to give the appearance of concen-
trating on algae and fungi so that she would not
attract Mr. Ericson's attention. Actually, she was con-
sidering the implications of the words, "Hi, Webfoot." For one thing, they told her that Philip had
read the interview. But Webfoot? Did Philip, like
Mr. Ericson, mean to be sarcastic? No, she was sure

he did not. He had sounded as if he were teasing in a friendly way.

Shelley clamped a slide under her microscope and prepared to draw a picture of a protococcus. Philip would never be sarcastic like Mr. Ericson. She turned the knob that adjusted the microscope and peered through the finder with her right eye until the one-celled plant came into focus. Then she looked through the microscope with her left eye and at the same time tried to look at her paper with her right eye. Mr. Ericson said that was the proper way to use a microscope, but Shelley felt as if her eyes were going off in different directions. To rest them she let both eyes stray to Philip.

"Shelley," said Mr. Ericson, "can you tell us how fission plants differ from thallus plants?"

"Um . . ." said Shelley, taken by surprise. "A fission plant . . . I'm sorry. I don't know."

"Philip?" asked Mr. Ericson.

"No, sir," answered Philip. "I don't know."

Jeannie knew. Quick, bright-eyed Jeannie always knew the answers.

Somehow Shelley got through the rest of the laboratory period. As she put away her microscope and closed her notebook, Philip turned to her with his lopsided grin and said, "So long, Webfoot." As usual, he left the room with Frisbie.

"Aren't boys maddening?" asked Jeannie sympathetically.

"Yes," agreed Shelley, and decided she had better forget about Philip before she became the laughing-stock of the whole school—if she was not already. She was ashamed of what she had done. When Philip was interviewed he had not said he liked her. Frisbie had said it for him, perhaps meaning it as a joke which she had been foolish enough to take seriously because she had wanted it to be true. She had been so sure that life in San Sebastian was going to be perfect and now she had made a mess of everything.

That afternoon after school Shelley wrote a long letter to her mother and father, telling them about her studies and the success of the doughnut-hole sale and the fun she was having with the Michies.

When she had sealed the letter she started a second letter. "Dear Rosemary, San Sebastian is simply perfect! And guess what? Remember that cute boy I told you about who sits next to me in biology? Well, now he calls me Webfoot! How's that for a nickname?" Shelley did not really feel the enthusiasm she was displaying in her letter, but she felt that since she had written so much about Philip in a previous letter to her best friend, she should mention him again. Webfoot was really not a promising nickname. A boy who liked a girl a lot would not call her Webfoot. Because Philip was important to her, she did not even think of him as Phil. He was Philip, and if she were important to him he would call her Shelley. Webfoot was a nickname for a girl who was a pal. Well, she didn't want to be a pal to Philip. She might as well forget him as she had decided once before that afternoon. Slowly Shelley tore the letter to bits and sprinkled the pieces into the wastebasket.

At supper that evening Katie announced, "Shelley was interviewed in the *Bastion*. I was looking at Luke's paper and I saw the interview."

"Oh, that silly thing," said Shelley hastily. She was not anxious to have Tom's and Mavis's attention called to her bad judgment. Mavis might even feel she had to speak to Shelley about it.

"Shelley said she liked basketball players who take biology," persisted Katie. "And they put it in the paper. And you know what? Philip Blanton plays basketball and takes biology!"

Shelley felt herself blushing. She was thoroughly ashamed of the example she had set Katie. She glanced at Tom and Mavis, who did not seem particularly concerned with the turn of the conversation. Mavis, with two children of her own, could not concern herself with Shelley's small problems. It was different at home, where Shelley's mother had only one child to think about. "Katie, I shouldn't have said what I did," said Shelley. "It was a stupid thing to do and I'm sorry I said it and I'm sorry they printed it."

"Just the same," said Katie dreamily, "I hope I get interviewed for the paper when I get to high school."

Tom turned to his son. "Well, Luke, what's this I hear about your having trouble in English?" he asked.

"It isn't fair!" Luke burst out. "Other kids don't have dads who teach at the same school they go to and hear every single little old thing that happens!"

"What did happen?" asked Tom.

Luke scowled at his plate.

"Yes, Luke, tell us," Mavis urged.

"Aw . . . the teacher wrote a bunch of sentences on the blackboard before class and then during class she went right down the row and asked each of us to read a sentence aloud and put the punctuation in," Luke explained. "When I came to my sentence I didn't want to do it, is all," said Luke.

"Why not?" asked Mavis. "Didn't you know how to punctuate it?"

"Sure I did," answered Luke, "but I knew if I read it all the kids would laugh. They laughed anyway."

"What was the sentence?" Tom asked jovially. "You can tell us. You're among friends."

Luke spoke rapidly, and without expression. " 'Mother,' I cried, 'they've crowned me Queen of the May.' "

Shelley could not help it. A shout of laughter escaped her along with the laughter of the rest of the family.

"See?" said Luke bitterly. "What did I tell you?"

The family made an effort to control its amusement. "Did you finally read it?" asked Mavis.

"She made me," said Luke. "And then she said I got it right except that if I had been crowned Queen of the May I would be excited and so it should be Queen of the May exclamation point. Boy, that really slayed the class."

Poor Luke. Shelley sympathized with him even though she could scarcely keep from laughing. She remembered how she had felt that afternoon when she was called "the late Shelley Latham."

"Luke, do the best work you can and try to be patient with your English teacher," said Mavis gently. "She obviously doesn't have a sense of humor and that is something she can't help."

"Mother, they've crowned me Queen of the May exclamation point!" said Katie dramatically.

"Now, Katie," warned Tom, "Luke has had enough trouble with that sentence."

"You know what we had to cook in cooking class today?" asked Katie. "Mush and breakfast cocoa." She made an expressive gagging noise. "And right after lunch, too."

Shelley studied the faces around her. The interview no longer seemed so important. This was one of the things she enjoyed most about living with a larger family. When she became absorbed in a prob-

lem, someone else came along with another problem and somehow her difficulty lost its importance.
At home all her problems were the center of interest.

Saturday morning after breakfast Tom and Luke
went out to work in the grove. Mavis went to her
studio over the garage and Shelley decided to run
the vacuum cleaner in her room. She even moved the
bed and was cleaning in the corner when Katie burst
into the room.

"Hi," said Shelley, switching off the vacuum cleaner.

"Shelley!" exclaimed Katie, who was plainly trying
to suppress great excitement. "Come down the road
with me. I want to show you something."

"What do you want to show me?" asked Shelley.

"It's a surprise," said Katie. "Shelley, you've got
to come!"

"All right," agreed Shelley, to please Katie. "How
far down the road?"

"Not very far," said Katie. "Get a bicycle and
come on."

The two girls, accompanied by Sarge, bicycled
down the road that bordered the grove and as they
pedaled, Katie chattered. "I can hardly wait until
tonight," she confided. "The dancing class that meets
at school once a month is having a hat dance."

"A hat dance?" asked Shelley. "I thought a hat
dance was a Mexican folk dance where the man
throws his hat on the floor and stamps his feet around
it."

Katie giggled. "Not this kind. It is our regular
dancing class, only everybody is supposed to concoct
some sort of château to wear and there will be prizes
for the best ones," answered Katie.

Shelley found this statement puzzling. "Oh, you
mean chapeau," she said, when she had figured out
Katie's meaning.

"Well, anyway, a crazy hat," said Katie. "Mine is a secret. Wait till you see it. I know it will win a prize."

"Is there some special boy you like?" asked Shelley.

"Could be," answered Katie mysteriously.

The two girls approached a house that was protected by a windbreak of eucalyptus trees and as they came near the trees, Shelley heard the sound of sawing.

"Look!" cried Katie triumphantly. "Up there in the wild blue yonder!"

Against the blue sky fifty feet above the ground and half hidden by leaves was Philip. He was leaning away from the tree, his body supported by a lineman's belt buckled around the trunk, his spiked heels digging into the wood. For a moment Shelley stood staring up, motionless in surprise, before she collected her thoughts and decided to leave quickly before Philip saw her.

From another treetop Frisbie's voice called out, "Hey, Phil! Here's the late Miss Latham!"

Philip stopped sawing at a branch and called down, "Hi, Webfoot!"

"Hi." Shelley had to answer, but she was sure that Philip would think she had found out where he was working and had deliberately ridden out to see him. She realized now, when it was too late, that she should have insisted upon Katie's telling her what the surprise was. Now, after that silly interview in the paper, Philip would think she was as persistent as—as a bloodhound. Not only had she tracked him down, now she had him treed. Well, she had no intention of sitting there baying at him. "Come on, Katie, let's go," she whispered.

"No, let's watch," begged Katie.

"Katie, please!" Shelley's whisper was urgent. Just wait till she got Katie alone! There were a few things she was going to explain to her.

Philip wiped the dust and sweat from his forehead with the back of his hand and went on sawing. The branch broke through and came crashing to the ground in a cloud of dust and a flutter of dry leaves. The sudden loss of the branch made the treetop spring back and forth and in spite of herself Shelley watched, fascinated. Philip looked so tall and strong up there in the swaying treetop.

"Katie," Shelley whispered, turning her bicycle around. "You can stay if you want to, but I'm leaving."

"But you said you liked him." Katie sounded hurt.

"Katie, you don't understand." Shelley mounted her bicycle. "I'll explain later."

"Hey, Webfoot," Frisbie called from a treetop. "Stick around. Phil wants to talk to you."

"Aw, shut up, Friz," Shelley heard Philip say in an undertone.

"Go on, ask her," said Frisbie.

"Sorry, Friz," Shelley called. "I have things to do." She gave what she hoped was a jaunty wave and started down the road.

"Shelley, wait!" Philip yelled, loud enough for the whole countryside to hear. "I want to talk to you."

This from shy Philip? Shelley hesitated, stopped, and looked back up at Philip, who was working his way down the tree trunk. He had called her Shelley so perhaps he meant what he said. She felt confused and, under Katie's interested eye, uncomfortable. Darn Katie, anyway.

"You heard the boy," shouted Frisbie from his treetop.

"You keep out of this, Friz," said Philip, unfastening the belt and jumping to the ground.

Shelley hesitated. After the way she had behaved she did not want to appear to pounce on him. On the other hand, she really did want to talk to him —terribly. Philip approached her, and even though he was dirty and sweaty he looked clean and healthy underneath the dirt and more wonderful than any boy Shelley had ever known.

"Shelley, may I come over this evening?" he asked.

When Shelley did not answer immediately, Katie whispered, "Go on. Say yes."

Shelley did not dare hesitate any longer, because there was no telling what Katie would take into her head to say or do. "Yes, I would love to have you come over," Shelley answered.

"Swell," said Philip. "I'll be over about eight."

"I'll see you then," answered Shelley, and pedaled down the road. She did not want to linger and appear too anxious, especially when she was so excited that her hands would have trembled if she had not been gripping the handle bars so tightly. She finally had a date with Philip.

Katie rode along beside her. "I knew he would ask you for a date," she said happily. "I just knew it."

"Katie—" began Shelley, and stopped because she did not know what to say. It was difficult to scold someone who was so happy for her and she did not know how to explain to Katie that although she was delighted to have a date with Philip, she felt she had done all the wrong things. After all, she was supposed to be a good experience for a girl who had reached a difficult age. She did not want Katie to think a girl should advertise in the school paper that she liked a boy and then go out and tree him. She should try to set the younger girl a good example and so far she had done a poor job. "Katie, it is nice of you to want me to have a date with Philip," she said tactfully, "but I am afraid he will think I chased him, especially after that awful interview I gave the school paper."

"But it worked," Katie pointed out.

"I know," admitted Shelley, thinking that this was what made it so difficult to explain. "But a girl really shouldn't run after a boy—at least not so he knows she is running after him."

"I suppose not," said Katie thoughtfully, as they turned into the Michies' driveway, "but just the same, I'm glad he's coming over to see you. Aren't you terribly excited? I would be."

Shelley laughed. "Yes, I'm excited," she admitted, in a voice much calmer than the feelings behind it. At the same time she wondered how she was going to keep Katie off the top of the refrigerator.

Chapter 6

That evening, as soon as the dishes were washed, Shelley ran upstairs to wash her face and change into a fresh cotton dress, one that she had not worn to school. She brushed her hair, applied her lipstick with care, and because this was such a special occasion, dusted powder across her nose. Glancing at her watch, she was disappointed to find she still had an entire hour to wait before Philip would ring the doorbell. One long hour. She could write to her mother and father, but she felt too excited to sit down with pen and paper. She twirled around to see how far her skirt would stand out. This made it necessary to comb her hair all over again, a task that used up only a few seconds of the hour. She sat carefully on her bed so that she would not wrinkle her skirt. Fifty-three minutes to Philip. Fifty-three crawling minutes. How could she ever live fifty-three minutes?

"Mom! Dad! Shelley!" yelled Katie from the living room. "Come and see my hat for the hat dance!"

Shelley, glad of a way to use up part of the fifty-three minutes, went downstairs, to see the hat that Katie had spent the afternoon creating in secrecy in the laundry.

Now Katie stood admiring herself in the mirror in the front hall. Upside down on her head was a hollowed-out head of curly chicory so large it covered almost all of her hair. Fastened here and there to the lettuce, were radishes and green onions. Sticking out of the back like two enormous hatpins were a wooden salad fork and spoon. The whole creation was anchored by two green ribbons tied under Katie's chin. "I'm a tossed green salad!" she announced.

Tom and Mavis shouted with laughter and Shelley thought Katie looked like a robust sprite. Luke, sitting in an easy chair with a pile of science-fiction magazines on the floor beside him, groaned and said, "Oh, for dumb!"

"Katie, that is priceless," said Mavis. "How did you ever think of such a thing?"

"I've always thought this kind of lettuce looked like curly green hair," said Katie.

"Mom, you don't mean you are going to let her go out in that thing, do you?" demanded Luke.

"Of course," answered Mavis. "I think it is fetching."

"Well, I think it looks dumb," said Luke. "Do we have to eat it after she gets through wearing it?"

"No, you don't," said Katie. "I bought the lettuce and radishes and onions with my own money. I didn't get them out of the salad things in the refrigerator."

"Come on, green salad," said Mavis, picking up the car keys from the mantel. "You don't want to be late."

"Have fun and I hope you get lots of dances with the right boy," said Shelley sincerely. If it hadn't been for Katie, she might not be waiting for Philip this very minute.

"He can graze on her hat while they dance," remarked Luke, from behind his magazines.

"Oh, be quiet," said Katie cheerfully, as she went

out the front door. She was too happy to be annoyed by anything her brother said.

Shelley rather envied Katie her puppyish excitement. She was excited too, but at sixteen a girl had learned to be more cautious about letting her feelings show until she knew for sure that a boy really liked her.

"Now, Luke," said Mavis. "Shelley is to have the living room this evening if she wants it."

"O.K.," said Luke without looking up.

Shelley smiled to herself. Not only was Philip coming to see her, she was going to have the living room all to herself when he came. This time she would not have to cringe inside, the way she always had when she introduced a boy to her mother and father and could feel them looking him over, wondering what his family was like and what his father did and what time he would bring her home. This time was going to be different.

Shelley was restless when Mavis and Katie had gone. Tom went outdoors and she was left alone with Luke. She glanced at the clock and wandered around the room, reading titles in the bookcase, picking up magazines and laying them down again. She wondered if Philip would walk or come in a car and what they would do when he arrived. Making a date with Katie present was not very satisfactory, because a boy naturally would not like to discuss the details with a younger girl hanging on every word he said. Whatever they did, she wanted more than anything for him to have a good time so that he would ask her out again and then again. It would be such fun to have dates with a boy all the girls wanted to know and especially during basketball season. She would go to all the games and when Philip scored everyone sitting near her would look at her and think, There's

Phil Blanton's girl, and she would go on cheering just as if she wasn't aware that everyone was looking at her. . . .

Shelley hummed to herself, nibbled at a hangnail, sat down. She wished Luke would hurry up and leave the room. It was not like him to spend the evening reading when he could be working on his motorcycle. And she still had Katie to worry about. If Katie came home and climbed up on the refrigerator again, perhaps she should look her straight in the eye through the glass in the transom and say, "Well, if it isn't Katie!" Maybe that would embarrass her enough to make her scramble down. There were, Shelley decided, a number of advantages to being an only child, after all. She hoped that Tom would not suddenly announce that this was a good night to wash or iron. It would never do to ask a star basketball player to help with the Michies' laundry.

Shelley looked at her watch again, stood up, read a few more titles in the bookcase, wandered across the room, and picked up one of Luke's science-fiction magazines.

"Luke, why do you read this stuff anyway?" Shelley asked, hoping to draw his attention from the story so that he might think about leaving.

"Because I like it," answered Luke, not looking up from his magazine.

Because she had to do something to fill the dragging minutes, Shelley read a few sentences to herself, giggled, and began to read aloud with exaggerated expression. " 'The sun beat down on the asteroid. Sweat stood out on the lean jaws of Brad Conway as he stared at the dials of the transmutor. In thirty seconds . . . in twenty seconds . . . in—' "

"Aw, cut it out," said Luke, looking up at last.

Amused that she had finally caught Luke's attention, Shelley dropped the magazine and picked up another, which she opened at random and began to read. " 'The spaceship left the planet and was only thirty light years into the galaxy when Captain Rowley felt the controlcomp go dead in his hands. Automatically he glanced earthside in the telescan—' "

The magazine was snatched from Shelley's hands. "You cut that out!" ordered Luke, so fiercely that Shelley was taken aback. These stories, which were funny to her, were not funny to him.

"I guess I was just surprised to see you reading, is all," Shelley faltered. "You're usually working on your motorcycle."

"Aw, Mom's right," said Luke morosely. "I'll never get it to run."

So that was what was bothering Luke. He was discouraged about his motorcycle. "Yes, you will," said Shelley, wanting him to succeed. "I know you will get it to run sometime."

The twirl of the doorbell was so startling to Shelley that she felt as if everything inside her had stopped. Philip! He had come and now she felt completely unprepared. Nervously she ran her hand over her hair and smoothed her skirt. What on earth would she say? She moistened her lips and with a hand chilled by nervousness, opened the door. Philip really was standing on the doorstep.

"Hello, Shelley," he said.

"Hello, Philip," answered Shelley. "Won't you come in?"

As Philip stepped through the door, Shelley saw that Luke had disappeared with his magazines. Uncertainly she asked Philip to sit down. She sat down on the opposite end of the couch. She found she could not look directly at him and so, instead, she stared at the toe of her shoe as if it were some strange new object she had never seen before. It was ridiculous to feel so embarrassed, she knew, and for a moment she could not understand why she felt that way. A first date was usually a little awkward but not this awkward, although, of course, none of her other first dates had been with Philip Blanton. Then Shelley realized she felt awkward because she was alone with him. Always before, the first moments had been spent introducing the new boy to her mother and father. She had never enjoyed the introductions, but at least introducing a boy had given her something definite to do for those first few moments. Now she was face to face with Philip, alone and on her own. She almost wished Tom would appear and say it was a good night to iron and why didn't they all pitch in and help?

Bravely Shelley looked at Philip and was rewarded by the lopsided grin. Encouraged, she said, "I was certainly surprised to see you up in that tree when Katie asked me to go bicycling this morning." That would show him that she had not intended to track him down.

"You saw the firm of Blanton and Gerard, Contractors, at work," said Philip. "We were cutting some of the branches before they got big enough to overhang the house. Eucalyptus is brittle in hot weather and sometimes the branches fall."

"Aren't you scared to climb such a high tree?" asked Shelley.

"No," said Philip. "I like it. I feel so sort of—well, I don't know—free, I guess, when I am up there."

"Do you get many jobs cutting branches?" asked Shelley, who until now had known only boys who earned money mowing lawns or washing cars.

"Some," answered Philip. "Friz and I cut trees, too, if they aren't too big. His dad lets us use his chain saw and we cut them up into fireplace lengths and then split them. You have to split eucalyptus wood as soon as it is cut or it gets too hard."

"You do?" said Shelley, admiring Philip and thinking that the sunburn on his nose the first day of school must have come from splitting wood under the California sun.

Conversation died. Philip and Shelley both looked down, looked at one another, and looked away, embarrassed that their eyes had met. For the first time Shelley noticed that the old clock on the mantel had an unusually loud tick.

Shelley could think of no way to revive the conversation. She had to do something, but what? The television set was not working and the Michies had not bothered to have it repaired. They did not have a record collection. Feeding a boy was always acceptable, but it was too early in the evening. Maybe she should suggest making fudge, the way teen pages in magazines recommended girls should entertain boys. They would have to wait for the fudge to cool and that would take time. But somehow Shelley did not feel she could ask a star basketball player to step into the kitchen to whip up a batch of fudge the minute he entered the house. Lots of boys she had known at home would make fun of a girl if she made such a suggestion. They would laugh about it by the lockers in the halls at school. Shelley did not really think that Philip, who was so reserved and had such nice manners, was that unkind but she did not want to suggest something he would merely be polite about. She wanted him to enjoy himself because she wanted him to come back. Why, *why* hadn't she thought of this problem before he came? *Tick, tick, tick* went the clock relentlessly. She had wasted the whole afternoon floating around in a happy glow wondering what she should wear, when she should have been planning something to do. *Tick, tick, tick.* Precious minutes were slipping away.

Shelley was actually relieved when the front door opened, Mavis entered, and she was no longer alone with Philip.

"Good evening, Mrs. Michie," said Philip, rising to his feet.

"Hello, Philip," said Mavis. "Shelley, I'm going out to my studio to work until I pick up Katie at eight-thirty. And by the way, there is a table tennis set in the bottom drawer in the dining room. It fits on the dining-room table."

Saved, thought Shelley, saved from the awful ticking of that clock. "Would you like to play table tennis?" she asked Philip.

Finding the set and clamping the net to the painted table gave them something to do, and while they worked Shelley thought of the mahogany dining table at home and how carefully her mother always wiped up the pollen that fell on its polished surface from the flowers in the centerpiece. They could never have played ping-pong on that table.

Shelley and Philip selected paddles and began to warm up with a few practice strokes. Philip served to Shelley, who missed. She had to get down on her hands and knees to retrieve the ball from underneath the table and as she got up, she bumped her head. She hit the ball back to Philip but it missed the table. Philip caught it easily in his hand and quickly served it back to Shelley. This time she managed to hit the ball into the net. Philip expertly scooped it up with his paddle and hit it toward Shelley once more.

This time I'm going to do it right, thought Shelley with determination, and swatted the ball as hard as she could. It flew across the net, hit the table, bounced up against the ceiling, dropped to the floor, and rolled into the kitchen, where Philip had to lie on his stomach on the floor to retrieve it from under the refrigerator.

Shelley laughed nervously. A star athlete, and she was pitting her skill against him. Shelley Latham, the girl who took physical education only because it was required.

Philip served to Shelley a ball so gentle that she was able to return it. "Let's start playing," he suggested, and served another easy ball for Shelley to return.

The restrained game continued, the ball bouncing gently back and forth across the net. Twice Shelley missed and had to chase the ball into the hall and once she overshot the table with her serve and Philip had to poke the ball out from under a chair with his paddle. Shelley was filled with humiliation. The county's star basketball player playing a ladylike game for her sake, letting her win points. He must be bored stiff.

The game finally ended with Philip winning, 21-18. "Your serve," he said, starting another game.

Grimly Shelley applied her paddle to the ball. Philip was being nice to her, but nice was not what she wanted him to be. Not in this way. She wanted him to have fun. *Plonk, plonk* went the ball on the dining-room table. This was like asking an All-American quarterback to enter a hopscotch contest. Shelley stole a glance at her watch. Katie would be home before long, and that was another problem. There was no telling what Katie would do or say except that whatever it was, it would be enthusiastic and most likely all wrong. Katie would probably walk in wearing her lettuce hair and say, right out loud, "That's not a very exciting game you are playing."

Plonk, plonk, plonk. Somehow Shelley got through

the second game, and smiled brightly at Philip in an effort to make him think she had enjoyed herself. She felt hot and flushed while he did not look as if he had been exercising at all.

Philip laid his paddle on the table. "I don't have the car," he said, "but if you don't mind walking we could go downtown for something to eat."

"That would be fun," said Shelley, who felt that anything would be better than batting that plonking little ball back and forth. After they had put away the net and paddles, Shelley led the way out the back door toward the garage. "I had better tell someone where I am going," she explained. They found Tom working on the engine of the station wagon, which was parked under a light on the front of the garage. "We're going to walk downtown for something to eat," said Shelley.

"Hello, Phil," said Tom. "Why don't you take our old tandem instead of walking?"

Shelley was aghast. A tandem *bicycle*? Only the Michies would own such a thing.

"Sounds like fun," said Philip. "How about it, Shelley?"

"Why . . . yes, it does sound like fun," Shelley agreed, with as much enthusiasm as she could muster. From one set of muscles to another, she thought. At least Philip was getting exercise even if he wasn't having any fun.

But riding the tandem was surprisingly easy. Shelley felt almost as if they were floating as they rode past the orange groves and down San Sebastian's wide main street. The night was soft and fragrant. Cars full of high-school students were cruising up and down the street, the boys and girls apparently having nothing better to do than ride around seeing what everyone else was doing. They tooted and yelled at one another

and when they saw Philip and Shelley, they sang
out, "On a bicycle built for two." It was a small-town
Saturday night, a new experience for Shelley. Philip
seemed to be enjoying himself. Shelley marveled that
she was riding down the main street on a tandem
behind the straight, slim back of Philip Blanton, the
shy boy whom all the girls wanted to date.

And to Shelley, the most wonderful part of it was
that such an experience could never have happened
at home. Nobody she knew owned a tandem, and
even if someone did, she could not imagine two high-
school students riding it in the evening on a date.
Anyway, at this time of year it would probably be
raining and if she went out with a boy who did not
have a car, she would have to wear galoshes. Free of
galoshes, Shelley felt light as air as she coasted through
the night, and as she coasted she made a resolution.
Never in the state of California, no matter how hard
it rained, if it ever did rain, would she wear galoshes.
Never.

Downtown, Shelley was surprised by the crowds
of people walking up and down the sidewalks and
by the number of cars looking for parking places.
She had forgotten that in San Sebastian stores were
open on Saturday night. Philip and Shelley parked
the bicycle in the rack in front of a small restaurant
and soda fountain called the Chicken Coop. The place
was crowded and the jukebox was blaring. Another
couple was leaving so they were fortunate to get a
booth beside the jukebox near the front door. As they
sat down at the table, littered with empty milk-shake
glasses, crumpled napkins, and paper coverings from
straws, Shelley looked around her. The walls were
papered with a design of mother hens each leading
four chicks repeated all the way around the restaurant;
the hens and chicks appeared to be marching in end-

less processions, around and around. Planting boxes were filled with artificial plants and behind the counter a pair of metal arms revolved continually in a plastic vat of orange juice. In the next booth a weary mother tried to appease two tired children with ice-cream sodas.

"What will you have?" asked Philip above the noise.

"A chocolate malt," answered Shelley. It was then that Shelley saw Katie and her mother sitting on stools eating ice-cream sodas. Katie was slowly spooning the ice cream out of the bottom of her soda. Dejection showed in the way she sat on the stool, the way she put the spoon in her mouth and pulled it out again half full of ice cream. Mavis was looking at Katie with a mixture of sympathy and irritation and Shelley knew she wanted to say, "Katie, don't eat your ice cream that way," but because of Katie's mood she was restraining herself.

So Katie had not had a good time at the dancing class she had looked forward to with such eagerness. Shelley was sorry. She had really wanted Katie to have a good time, because she liked Katie and because she was grateful to her for her own date with Philip.

A waitress appeared to clear off the table and take Shelley's and Philip's orders. "Two chocolate malts and a grilled peanut-butter sandwich," said Philip.

"A grilled *peanut-butter* sandwich!" Shelley could not help exclaiming. She had never heard of such a thing.

"I'm hungry," explained Philip.

When the waitress had gone, Shelley raised her voice above the noise and said, "I was surprised when you came down from the top of that tree to ask me for a date." The record on the jukebox ended suddenly and Shelley found herself speaking the last words for everybody to hear.

Philip flashed his wonderful grin. "Maybe I should have swung from branch to branch yelling my bull-ape cry like Tarzan."

Shelley giggled. "That really would have surprised me." Shelley saw Mavis pay for the sodas and leave the counter with Katie. "Hi," Shelley called out, when they reached the door.

"Oh, hello there," said Mavis, as Philip rose awkwardly to his feet behind the table.

"Hi," said Katie without expression. Whatever was wrong must be very wrong indeed, if Katie could not look admiringly at Philip.

Mavis lowered her voice. "We needed a little something to cheer us up," she said as they went out the door.

"What's the matter?" asked Philip as he sat down and picked up his grilled peanut-butter sandwich.

"It's Katie," said Shelley. "Something awful must have happened at her dancing class."

"Kids that age—" said Philip, leaving his remark unfinished as if whatever he had in mind was such common knowledge that he did not need to say it. The mechanical arm of the jukebox picked another record out of the stack, dropped it into place, and the voices of a quartet boomed forth.

The door opened. "Hey, Wilma," a man startled Shelley by yelling to the waitress. "Charlie been in yet?"

"Nope. Not yet," the waitress yelled back.

Philip, used to the ways of a small town, did not appear to notice the interruption. "I wanted to ask you for a date sooner," he confessed, in the lull between records on the jukebox, "but I—I couldn't."

Puzzled, Shelley wanted to ask what had prevented

him, but she felt that she should not pry. Perhaps he meant that he did not have the courage, although he did not seem excessively shy, since he had asked her for a date in front of Katie. Some boys would not have done that. "I hope you didn't mind what I said to the Roving Reporter," she said, not really wanting to bring up the matter, but feeling that she must because she still felt guilty about it.

"Oh, that," said Philip, and laughed. "I hope you didn't mind what Friz said about you."

The sound of a slap and the wail of a child came from the next booth. "Charlene, I *told* you not to put sugar cubes in your soda without taking the wrappers off." The woman's voice was tired and sharp. "Just for that I'm not going to buy you no water pistol."

Shelley lowered her eyes and pulled the wrapper off the straw the waitress had laid in front of her. "No. I—I was pleased by what Friz said," she admitted, and stirred the milk shake with her straw. The jukebox blared again, making conversation across the table almost impossible. Well, anyway I am with him, thought Shelley, wishing she could put a nickel in the jukebox and buy five cents' worth of silence. If only they could talk she might find some sign that he was having a good time—or not having a good time. It was the suspense of not knowing that was so hard to bear.

When Philip pulled the tandem out of the rack and they started home, Shelley discovered why riding downtown had been so easy. It had been downhill all the way, because San Sebastian was built on the gentle slope at the front of the mountains. And now the way home was uphill. Shelley pushed harder on the pedals, because it did not seem fair to let

Philip do all the work. The street was steeper than
it looked.

"This is the widest main street I have ever seen,"
said Shelley, managing not to puff.

"The men who planned San Sebastian way back
planned it that way so they could turn a span of
eight mules," explained Philip, with no sign of a
puff.

"Oh," said Shelley, tempted to let her aching legs
coast around with the pedals. "That's interesting."
The slope seemed to grow steeper with every turn
of the pedals.

When Philip stood up on the pedals to exert more
pressure on them, Shelley listened for some sign that
he, too, was out of breath. His wind was excellent.
A line of verse that she had read someplace a long
time ago pushed its way into Shelley's thoughts. She
could not recall it exactly, but it was something about,
"Does the road go uphill all the way? Yes, to the very
end." It was a perfect description of San Sebastian's
main street.

Shelley gathered all the breath she could spare and
said, "It's such a beautiful night." She hoped that
from then on her silence would be taken for a rapt
appreciation of the stars shining down on San Sebastian.

Fortunately the road was level when they turned off
the main street, and Shelley partially caught her
breath before they turned into the Michies' driveway. While they parked the tandem in the garage
and walked around to the front door, Shelley wondered uneasily what Katie was doing. She opened
the front door, and before she turned to face Philip
she glanced at the transom at the end of the living
room. Katie was not in sight. "Well . . . good night,
Philip," Shelley said uncertainly. A first good night

was so terribly important. It could mean the beginning of so many things or it could mean—good night.

Philip smiled down at Shelley. "You're a good sport," he said.

Encouraged, Shelley said, "I'm not much of a ping-pong player, but I had fun anyway."

"So did I," said Philip. "Say, Shelley, I was wondering—would you like to go to Vincente to the movies next week end?"

"I'd love to, Philip," said Shelley happily. So he had had a good time after all! The suspense had ended. Now she knew.

"Swell," said Philip. "I'll see you at school. Good night."

"Good night, Philip." Shelley silently closed the door. Philip Blanton had asked her for another date! The polite table-tennis game, the pulling ride home seemed unimportant. He liked her, she liked him, and Katie had not been on top of the refrigerator. Shelley climbed the creaking stairs as quietly as she could and at the door of her room she hesitated. A strip of light shone beneath the door of Katie's room across the hall. Shelley waited a moment and then tapped on the door of Katie's room with one fingernail.

"Come in," answered Katie in a dull voice, and Shelley entered. Katie was leaning on her dresser, her chin propped on her fists, staring at herself in the mirror. Her mouth was heavily made up with dark lipstick.

"I suppose you had fun," said Katie in the same dull voice.

"A wonderful time." Shelley tried not to smile at the sight of Katie's mouth. Although she knew the answer, she asked, "Did you?"

"No," said Katie flatly.

"What went wrong?" asked Shelley.

"Everything," answered Katie, turning away from the mirror. "Just everything."

"Didn't the right boy dance with you?" asked Shelley.

"Dance with me!" exclaimed Katie. "He wasn't even there. Practically no boys came except some whose mothers made them come and you know that type."

"Yes, I know," said Shelley. "But why didn't the boys come? They usually turn up."

"They didn't want to make hats," said Katie. "They said it was too much bother. You know how boys are."

"Yes," agreed Shelley, sorry for her. "But didn't you win a prize for your hat?"

"No," said Katie. "Pamela did, though. She said she was going to make a hat out of a bird cage and instead she turned up in a straw hat with a little palm tree and a monkey on it. When she wound up the monkey it played a drum."

"I'm sure your hat was more becoming." Shelley tried to be comforting.

Katie sighed gustily. "What difference did it make, when I had to dance with girls? Do you think that this lipstick, not that Mommy would ever let me wear it, makes me look sophisticated?"

Shelley managed not to smile. "Well—not sophisticated exactly."

"It's just hopeless," said Katie. "I'm nothing but a wholesome outdoor type. The type that has to lead when there aren't enough boys to dance with. And it is horrible to be thirteen."

"Cheer up, Katie," Shelley said. "You won't stay thirteen all your life. After all, I was thirteen once."

"I guess that's right," said Katie, brightening. "But you don't know how lucky you are to be sixteen."

"Am I?" asked Shelley dreamily. "Well, good night, Katie." She went to her room and, without turning on the light, stood at the window looking out into the soft, dark night. She recalled how she had felt at thirteen. Nothing had seemed right. The girls were taller than the boys and at dancing class, even when there were enough boys to go around, the girls had really led, because the boys all seemed too confused to learn the steps. And clothes had never fitted properly. And at thirteen there never seemed to be anything to do, because at thirteen a girl is too old for toys and not old enough for dates. Now that she looked back on that age, Shelley knew that she was glad to be through with it, to have said good-by to so many things.

Shelley smiled in the darkness. Katie was right. She was lucky to be sixteen. She was the luckiest girl in San Sebastian, because she was sixteen and Philip Blanton liked her. Shelley was filled with a wonderful feeling of excitement as if something was about to happen, something more wonderful than anything that had ever happened before. Something magic.

Chapter 7

After Shelley's first date with Philip, each day seemed more golden and more spellbound. The sun shone and the sky was clear. The oranges were ripening. Violets and iris bloomed in November, Shelley discovered, and felt sorry for these poor confused California flowers that did not know they were supposed to bloom in the spring.

The leggy plants beside the back door put forth scarlet leaves and Shelley saw that these plants which she had thought so ugly were poinsettias. Poinsettias higher than her head! Until now she had seen them only in pots and thought that was the way they always grew.

At the same time the spreading gray-green tree that overhung the two-story garage began to burst with buds, clusters of tiny greenish-yellow balls, and Shelley discovered that this was an acacia tree. At home acacia blossoms were bought in bunches at the florist shop and she had supposed that an acacia was a small bush. As Shelley stood under the poinsettias and looked up at the acacia tree, she felt like Alice in Wonderland after she had drunk from the bottle labeled *Drink Me* and found everything the wrong size because she was shrinking. Yes, San Sebastian was a magic place.

And the most magic thing about Shelley's new life

was Philip. Whenever he saw her at school he smiled his slow grin, detached himself from the group of boys he was talking to, and came to smile down at her and say a few words while the other girls watched enviously. On Friday afternoons he had a way of seeming suddenly to remember that the next day was Saturday and of asking her for a date just when, after an agony of anticipation, she was sure he had forgotten. Sometimes they went to the movies and sometimes they played table tennis on the dining-room table. Although it was Philip whom she liked, and not Ping-Pong, Shelley found her game improving. Philip showed no interest in any other girl and Shelley, busy with her life at the Michies', was not interested in any other boy. She was completely happy.

Hartley, of course, Shelley saw every day, because he sat behind her in her registration room. Although their relationship had never been quite comfortable since they had said good night under the interested eye of Katie, he was always fun to talk to. Hartley was—well, good old Hartley.

One afternoon in biology lab, while Shelley and Jeannie and the two boys who sat beside them were getting their microscopes out of the cupboards and opening their notebooks, Jeannie said, "I'm in charge of decorating the gym for the barn dance. I hereby appoint the three of you to be on the committee. If we round up a bunch of others it shouldn't be too much work."

"I'd love to," said Shelley. This was one of the things she liked best about San Sebastian High. The chairman of a committee was formally appointed, but after that arrangements for school activities were casual and usually resulted in anyone's taking part who wanted to.

"You've talked me into it," Frisbie told Jeannie, "if you'll go to the dance with me."

"Of course," agreed Jeannie. "Why else would I ask you to be on the committee?"

"I thought maybe you wanted me for my muscles," said Frisbie, "to lift bales of hay or something."

"Maybe the four of us could double date," suggested Philip, his eyes on the rubber band he was playing with.

"I think that would be fun," said Shelley, delighted that for once Philip was asking her ahead of time.

"Well, what do you know!" exclaimed Frisbie. "Phil is finally going to break down and go to a school dance. After all these years."

"Aw—" muttered Philip.

Shelley could not help smiling to herself. It was nice to know she was to be the first girl Philip took to a school dance. It made her feel special.

"Does anybody know where we can borrow any authentic old wagon wheels?" asked Jeannie.

"There's one leaning against the front of practically every ranch house in town," said Frisbie. "Phil and I can probably round up a few."

Mr. Ericson interrupted the conversation. "If the cozy coterie at the table by the door will adjourn, we shall turn to the topic of the day—osmosis. Jeanne, will you please define osmosis?"

"Osmosis is the movement of molecules of water and dissolved substances through semipermeable membranes," answered Jeannie promptly.

For this she had Shelley's admiration. Shelley was sure that Jeannie's mind had been entirely on the dance. That was where Shelley's mind had been. Fortunately Mr. Ericson had not asked her the question.

The afternoon of the barn dance Philip come to

pick up Shelley in his father's car. In the back seat
was a pair of wagon wheels, each labeled with the
name of its owner.

"One of those wagon wheels is Pamela's mother's,"
said Katie, as she looked admiringly at Philip's green
sweater with the yellow block S and the yellow stripe
on the left sleeve. Katie always managed to be on
hand when Philip arrived and Shelley enjoyed showing him off "You'd better take good care of it. Pamela's mother had to look all over before she found it in
an antique shop. They are awfully hard to find."

"Don't worry," said Shelley. "We'll take good care
of the rare old antique."

As they drove to school, Shelley noticed that the
sky was more cloudy than she had ever before seen
it in San Sebastian. There had been a shower or two
since she had come to California and once it had
rained hard in the night, but this was the first time
that she had seen threatening rain clouds. She did
not know why she was surprised. It was really winter,
although to her, because there had been no autumn
leaves and no frost, it did not feel like winter. It did
not seem like any season at all and the brooding
clouds seemed out of place in the sky.

The clouds did produce rain, though, and suddenly.
Large drops spattered flatly against the car and all at
once rain was being dumped on San Sebastian. The
windshield wipers wagged furiously and then more
slowly, as if the weight of the unexpected rain was
too much for them.

Shelley rolled the window down a few inches.
"M-m-m," she breathed. "Smell the rain and feel the
wonderful damp air. I feel as if I were absorbing it
like a sponge." Now her hair would curl without so
much coaxing.

Philip laughed. "Maybe you'll begin to swell up,"

he said, as he parked the car near the gym under a pepper tree that made a lacy green curtain, shutting them off from the street. He turned off the windshield wipers. Rain beat down on the car and flowed down the windshield, blurring the outside world.

"Hi, Webfoot," Philip drawled, turning toward her.

"Hi." Shelley half whispered the syllable. They were so alone and Philip was so close. She was aware of him, clean and tan in his letter man's sweater, as she never had been before. She was aware of the rough wool of his sweater and the stripe on his sleeve just five stitches wide, the texture of the block S like thousands of tiny French knots, the clean white T shirt, the golden tan of his skin, that tiny mole just below his left ear lobe. . . . Shelley did not know why, but she felt frightened.

Philip took Shelley's hand in his. His hand was thin and hard, the way a boy's hand should be. "Shelley—" he began, and stopped.

Shelley managed to raise her eyes to his. She knew with a panicky feeling that he was about to kiss her.

Philip, lowering his eyes in his shy way, looked down at her hand in his. "Nothing," he said quietly. Slowly he released her hand. The moment was over.

Shelley realized she had been holding her breath and tried to let it out quietly so it would not sound like a sigh. Enclosed in the car, even with the rain beating on the roof, she was sure he could hear her breathe and perhaps hear her heart beat. She struggled to swallow without sounding as if she were gulping. It was funny how being alone with a boy and close to him could be so exciting and at the same time so embarrassing.

"Maybe we better run for it," she said reluctantly.

"I mean—we can't just sit here all afternoon, can we?"

"Maybe we better." There was reluctance in Philip's voice, too.

"It's awfully wet out." A silly thing to say, with the gutter running like a river.

"Yes. . . ." Philip was looking at her. She could feel it. "It's pretty wet."

All right. They agreed it was wet.

"Here." Philip pulled off his sweater. "You'd better wear my sweater or you'll get soaked. That sweater of yours is pretty thin."

"But what about you? You'll get wet." Philip's sweater was a temptation to Shelley.

"If I get too wet I have a sweat shirt in my locker in the gym." Philip draped his sweater around Shelley's shoulders.

"In that case, all right." Shelley slid her arms into the too-big sleeves, which made her feel fragile, like someone who needed to be protected from the elements. The wool, which was rough against her skin, smelled pleasantly of Philip.

Another couple ran past the car toward the gym. They were wearing slickers, and soldier hats folded out of newspaper. The girl, who carried her shoes in her hand, was barefooted.

"Wait till I get the wagon wheels out," said Philip, as he ducked out of the car.

Shelley followed him. The rain was cold against her face and legs but she did not care. She took one of the wagon wheels from Philip and together they raced, rolling the wheels like hoops ahead of them. They arrived at the door of the gym wet and laughing. Inside, the committee and Mr. Lutz, the teacher of commercial subjects and sponsor of the dance, were hard at work.

"Hi, there," called Jeannie. "Trickle in and go to work. We're leaning the wagon wheels around the bandstand."

Shelley ran her finger through her damp hair and looked around. Wires had been strung from one end of the gym to the other, and over the wires hung yards of blue cloth that hid the ceiling and hung down over the windows. Although the cloth did not succeed in looking like the sky, at least it diminished the gymnasium look, particularly in the dim light produced by the spotlights. Sheets of brown paper had been tacked up at the end of the gym, where members of the art class were painting barn scenes with poster paint.

A girl who was painting a row of cheerful, smiling cows stood back to look at her work. "Talk about contented cows," she said admiringly.

"They may be contented," said Frisbie, from the top of a stepladder where he was adjusting a spotlight, "but they are knock-kneed."

"It's the effect that counts," answered the girl.

Leaving a trail of wet footprints behind them, Shelley and Philip rolled their wagon wheels to the bandstand, where Jeannie and two other girls were making a scarecrow.

"I'm going to change into my sweat shirt," said Philip, and went off to the locker room.

Shelley was pleasantly aware that the other girls were looking at her in Philip's sweater with the sleeves pushed up above her elbows so they would stay up. Although it was not the custom in San Sebastian for a girl to wear a letter man's sweater (Shelley had found that out the first week of school), still there was something special about a boy's even lending a girl his sweater with a block letter—especially when the boy was Philip.

Philip came running out of the locker room in his
sweat shirt, dribbling an imaginary basketball. He
stopped, caught it, and made what was obviously a
difficult shot.

A cheer went up from the committee.

"Isn't that sweater awfully damp to be wearing
around?" asked one of the girls, whose name was
Arlene. She was in Shelley's English class and was
the kind of girl who enjoyed catching the teacher in
mistakes.

"Not especially," answered Shelley lightly. She did
not mind the girl's jealousy a bit. Not one little bit.
She went to work pinning a pair of garden gloves to
the scarecrow's sleeves.

"Hey, Friz," yelled one of the boys. "You're giving
us too much light."

"I'll fix it," Frisbie yelled back.

"Now wait a minute," said Mr. Lutz, coming over
to Frisbie's stepladder. "What we need is more light,
not less."

Voices rose in protest. "Aw, Mr. Lutz, nobody wants
to dance around in broad daylight!" "Aw, Mr. Lutz,
that's no fun." "Be a sport and let us dim them
some more."

"I'm prepared to be scientific about this." Mr. Lutz
pulled from his pocket a light meter, the kind ama-
teur photographers use, and held it up toward the
spotlight. "Sorry," he said, squinting at the red indi-
cator on the meter, "but the light meter has to read
one foot-candle for each spotlight. It's a rule." Then
he grinned. "I have to keep one step ahead of you
kids." The boys grumbled good-naturedly and went
back to work.

The afternoon went quickly for Shelley. Reluctantly she took off Philip's sweater, but not before
she was sure everyone had seen her wearing it. It was

such wonderful fun to be part of behind-the-scenes. This had never happened to her at home. She enjoyed every minute of the committee's clowning. One of the boys caught Arlene and put a dab of red poster paint on the tip of her nose while she squealed, "Let go! You're hurting me!" and everyone knew Arlene enjoyed it. And when it came time to sprinkle the special powder for dance floors on the floor of the gymnasium, Shelley joined the others in running and sliding. What fun she would have writing home about this! Dear Rosemary, she would write. I had the craziest afternoon. We were having a barn dance at school and Philip and I were on the committee. . . . Dear Mother and Daddy, This afternoon Philip and I helped decorate for the barn dance at school. He is such a nice boy. I know you would like him a lot. . . .

Finally, when the work was done and Mr. Lutz was off someplace seeing that the stepladders were put back where they belonged, Jeannie looked around thoughtfully. "I wish we had some hay," she remarked to Philip and Frisbie. "It doesn't seem like a real barn dance without a few bales of hay."

"That's easy," answered Frisbie. "I know where we can get some. You know that place up near the mountains that has the horses? I know the man who owns it."

"I never thought of that," said Jeannie. "Could you really get some?"

"Sure, if Phil will help," answered Frisbie. "We can load it into the station wagon and get it here in plenty of time. Phil and I will drive out and get the hay and pick you girls up half an hour early. That will give us time to bring the hay in before the crowd arrives."

Mr. Lutz began to turn out the lights in the gym,

and the few committee members left straggled toward the door. "Shelley, you look as if you thought something exciting was about to happen," remarked Jeannie, as she and Shelley paused in the doorway of the gym and looked out into the rain, which was now falling steadily.

"I'm going to the dance tonight," Shelley answered, remembering that Hartley had once made the same observation about her.

Jeannie looked curiously at her. "And you feel that a school dance is something to get excited about?" asked Jeannie.

"Of course," said Shelley. "Aren't you excited?"

"I suppose so." Jeannie sounded doubtful.

"But Jeannie, what is a dance for if it isn't fun and excitement?" Shelley wanted to know. To her a dance was an occasion, something to anticipate. She reminded herself that she was going with Philip and Jeannie was going with Frisbie, and that might make a difference.

Jeannie did not answer, because Philip and Frisbie joined the two girls and together they ran out through the rain to their cars.

The rain continued to fall and was still falling at seven-thirty, when Philip was to call for Shelley. She had, with concealed reluctance, returned his sweater to him when he had brought her home that afternoon. Now, when Philip twirled the doorbell, she realized she had to wear some kind of wrap. "Let him in, Katie, will you?" she called down the stairs. She always enjoyed showing Philip off to Katie, who quite plainly agreed that he was the most wonderful boy in San Sebastian.

Shelley snatched from her closet shelf a box that she had stuffed into her trunk unopened when she had packed and which had remained like that on her

closet shelf since she had come to California. From
the box she pulled the pink raincoat with the velveteen collar and the little hat with the black velveteen
button on top. Oh, well, she thought and slipped the
raincoat on over her blouse and full cotton skirt. She
put on the hat and patted the button on top while
she looked at herself in the mirror. It really was a
pretty raincoat.

Shelley drew the line, however, at galoshes. She
had vowed she would never wear galoshes in California, and she would not. But Shelley, she could
almost hear her mother say, you'll get your feet wet
and you'll ruin your shoes. But Mother, she could
hear herself answer, I'm in California now and I'm
not going to wear galoshes. I'll run quickly through
the rain, but I won't wear galoshes.

Philip was wearing jeans and a blue plaid shirt
under his letter man's sweater. "Hey, look at the
glamorous raincoat," he said when he saw her.

At the foot of the stairs Shelley twirled around
for his inspection before they ran out through the
rain to the station wagon. They slid into the second
seat in front of two bales of hay.

"Whew! It smells dusty in here," remarked Shelley.

"What a pretty raincoat," remarked Jeannie from
the front seat beside Frisbie. "Is that what they wear
up North?"

"Some people," answered Shelley, remembering the
front steps of school crowded with girls in slickers.
She discovered the price tag still dangling from one
sleeve. Carefully she untied it and put it in her pocket.
It was an expensive raincoat, more expensive than
her family could really afford. She was sorry she had
behaved the way she had.

"We'd better not let the hay get wet," said Frisbie. "Remember that hay Mr. Ericson soaked in water?"

"And we looked at a drop of the water under the microscope," added Jeannie. "It was swimming with all sorts of squirmy little things."

When they reached the gym they all climbed out of the station wagon. "Look!" exclaimed Jeannie, pointing. "I see a couple of stars over there. Maybe it is going to clear up after all."

As Philip and Frisbie dragged one of the bales of hay out of the station wagon and carried it up the steps of the gym, Frisbie sang, " 'Lift that barge, tote that bale,' " in his deepest voice. He pounded on the door and the janitor, who was turning on the lights, let them in. "Where do you want the hay, Jeannie?" Frisbie asked, while the janitor, protector of the gymnasium floor, eyed their wet feet with disapproval.

"Down at the end of the gym," directed Jeannie. "Did you bring some pliers?"

"Sure did," said Frisbie, pulling them out of his hip pocket and snapping the wire around the hay.

Jeannie and Shelley scattered the hay across the end of the gym while the boys carried in the second bale. By the time that bale was scattered, the orchestra had assembled, unpacked their instruments, and were blowing a few experimental notes.

Frisbie grabbed Jeannie and danced her around, singing at the top of his voice, " 'I want a buddy, not a sweetheart.' " They were an odd-looking couple. Frisbie was so big and Jeannie was so small.

Philip put his arm around Shelley, still in her raincoat, and began to dance with her to the tootling of the band. Shelley laughed and thought how different she would have felt at home. At home she would probably have slunk off to the checkroom the very first thing to get rid of the raincoat before anyone saw it. Here she did not care who saw it. That's funny, she thought. I wonder why.

The door of the gym opened and Mr. Lutz entered with a man in the uniform of the San Sebastian fire department. They stood looking around at the decorations. Then the man from the fire department saw the hay. "Has that hay been fireproofed?" he asked.

The two couples stopped dancing, "Why—no," confessed Jeannie, because she was chairman of the decorating committee.

"Where did it come from?" asked Mr. Lutz.

"We brought it, sir," said Philip.

"Who gave you permission?" demanded Mr. Lutz.

"Nobody," admitted Frisbie. "We didn't know we needed permission."

"It didn't seem like a barn dance without hay," explained Jeannie.

"So we drove up toward the mountains and got a couple of bales," continued Frisbie.

"Sorry," said the man from the fire department. "You'll have to get it out of here. It's a fire hazard."

"But nobody smokes at a school dance," protested Frisbie.

"That doesn't matter," said the man from the fire department. "It's still a fire hazard. You can't leave it here."

By this time couples were arriving and gathering around to see what the discussion was about.

"But what will we do with it?" asked Jeannie. There was a lot of hay in two bales.

"Take it out to the incinerator and burn it," said Mr. Lutz. "Every bit of it."

"In the rain?" asked Frisbie.

Mr. Lutz grinned. "You got it here in the rain,

didn't you? And anyway, the rain has just about stopped."

Frisbie and Jeannie groaned. The orchestra began to play and couples began to dance. "Now," said Mr. Lutz sternly. "I thought I had managed to stay one step ahead of you kids, but you put one over on me this time."

Shelley joined the others in gathering up armfuls of hay. " 'Lift that barge, tote that bale,' " Frisbie sang, and the other three joined in as they trooped toward the door of the gym. The rest of the crowd stopped dancing and began to clap hands to the rhythm of the song. The orchestra stopped what they had been playing and one by one the instruments took up the tune. The two couples, with their arms full of hay, splashed through puddles under the clearing sky and, while the fire inspector watched, threw the hay into the yawning cement mouth of the incinerator. They returned to the gym for a second load and then another and another. Everyone saw Shelley in her pink raincoat and the hat with the velveteen button on top, but she did not care. She thought the whole incident was funny, just one of those wonderful crazy things.

As Shelley made her way out the door of the gym with her last armful of hay, she found herself face to face with Hartley, who was entering with a girl from her English class. For some reason Shelley was startled. She had not expected to see Hartley at the dance and certainly not with that girl.

"Well, hello there," said Hartley.

"Hello," answered Shelley uncertainly. If Hartley wanted to bring that girl from her English class to the dance, there was no reason why he shouldn't, was there? Hartley and his date went on into the gym and Shelley went on out to the incinerator, trailing wisps of hay behind her.

The fire inspector had touched a match to the hay, which was burning merrily. "Too bad we don't have some marshmallows," said Frisbie, brushing hay from the sleeves of his sweater.

Philip stood close to Shelley and as she watched the sparks fly up and disappear into the night, she laughed from sheer happiness. Shelley felt Jeannie looking at her and knew that Jeannie was probably thinking wistfully that Shelley had fun in strange ways. Shelley did not care. Since she had come to San Sebastian everything had been fun, surprising and exciting. Even wearing the raincoat that had once caused her to stuff roses into the Disposall now seemed part of a delightful adventure. It almost seemed like magic, the way her feelings had changed.

And all at once Shelley understood why she was having such a good time in a raincoat she had once said she would never wear. When a girl comes to a school and makes a name for herself with a good idea and is interviewed for the school paper and liked by a boy all the other girls like—a boy who wanted to kiss her and who lets her wear his letter man's sweater while she decorates for a dance, it doesn't matter what kind of raincoat she wears. Any kind will do.

Chapter 8

When Christmas vacation arrived Shelley was surprised to learn that in California spruce and pines and even hemlocks were used for Christmas trees. She had always thought Christmas trees were Douglas fir, or they were not Christmas trees. She was even more surprised at the Michies' admiration for what was to her the ordinary holly wreath that her mother sent. They hung it on the front door and everyone who entered the house exclaimed, "Real English holly!" as if it were something rare and beautiful.

The days went quickly. There was shopping to do and packages to mail. Shelley helped Katie make a gathered skirt and spent hours watching Mavis at the potter's wheel in her studio. The spinning clay beneath her fingers was like a living thing. Shelley was fascinated. She experimented with a simple bowl and made up her mind that someday she would have a potter's wheel too.

There was a wonderful Christmas box from home, full of all the things a girl would like to receive— a new sweater and a matching skirt, a pretty scarf, two frilly slips, a bottle of perfume, a purse with a crisp five-dollar bill inside. Shelley could tell that her mother had found a lot of pleasure in packing that box. Christmas afternoon there was a long-distance call from home. Shelley was excited and a little sad to talk to her mother and father so far away.

And then New Year's Eve came. The Michies celebrated by inviting all the neighbors, young and old, for a buffet supper. Babies were bedded down, toddlers ran around in their sleepers, and grandparents were given the most comfortable chairs. Philip came too. He joined the crowd in making paper hats out of the crepe paper Mavis had supplied because she found paper hats for a crowd cost too much and decided it would be more fun and much less expensive if everyone made his own. Philip's hat looked something like a football helmet and a little like a baby's bonnet. Shelley thought it was the nicest party she had ever attended.

There was New Year's Day to be spent picking up after the party, and then vacation was over and it was time for school again. One damp day Shelley and Jeannie were eating their lunches in the study hall. From the window Shelley could see the top of an acacia tree in full bloom, each panicle a burst of fluffy balls of pure yellow. The blossoms were the essence of yellow and Shelley knew that whenever she thought of the color she would remember this sight—the soft blue-green foliage bending under the weight of raindrops and the sharp, clear yellow of the blossoms that somehow never looked wet no matter how hard it rained.

"Starry-eyed Shelley," remarked Jeannie.

"Am I starry-eyed?" asked Shelley, surprised.

"All the time," said Jeannie positively.

"If I am I guess it is because everything is so new and exciting down here," said Shelley, "but I don't really think I am starry-eyed."

"How you can find a dull little town like San

Sebastian exciting is a mystery to me," said Jeannie, stuffing the waxed paper wrapping from her sandwich into her brown paper bag. "I can't wait to leave it and go out into the world and find some excitement."

"Isn't that funny?" remarked Shelley. "I won't even let myself think about the time I have to leave it."

"You don't know how lucky you are," said Jeannie. "I would give anything to go to a big city high school and live in a town where there is something to do on Saturday night besides riding up and down the main street tooting at everyone else riding up and down the main street." She paused and wadded the brown paper bag into a tight ball. "I'm tired of living in a town where everyone knows everyone else's business, and I'm tired of living in a little house practically hidden by a clump of dusty pampas grass, and I'm tired of scorching-hot summers. Why, my family took a trip to Oregon once, and do you know what we saw? In downtown Portland on several street corners there were drinking fountains—each one was really four fountains made out of bronze or something—and the water ran *all the time!* There weren't even any handles so you could turn the water off."

Shelley laughed. "Why, that's true. I've seen those drinking fountains hundreds of times and I never thought a thing about them."

"I thought they were the most wonderful sight I had ever seen," said Jeannie. "All that lovely cold water."

Both girls were silent. Jeannie was occupied with her own rebellious thoughts. Shelley was thinking that this was the end of the semester. Half her precious months were already gone. "Report cards today," she remarked. "I wonder what the verdicts will be."

Jeannie did not appear to hear her. "Anyway," she remarked as they prepared to leave the study hall, "I'm not so sure it is San Sebastian that makes you starry-eyed." This time it was Shelley who did not appear to hear.

After the last class the students returned to their registration rooms to receive their report cards. When Shelley's grades were handed to her in a white envelope with her name typed in one corner, she accepted them with a nice feeling of accomplishment. One semester was behind her, another was about to begin. One by one she pulled out the cards for her different courses. A in English. A in Latin. Shelley always got A's in Latin, a language that she enjoyed because it seemed to her like a complicated puzzle. B in history. She had expected this—she was good at remembering dates, but this teacher had a way of wanting to know why historical events had taken place rather than when. Never mind, she would do better next semester. B minus in physical education. Field sports in this heat—she was lucky to get a B minus! D in biology.

Biology, D. It couldn't be! Shelley had never received a D in her life. Of course she realized she wasn't exactly at the head of the class, but D—why, Mr. Ericson could not do that to her. She wouldn't make the honor roll. She had to have a B average to get into college. She simply could not get a D; that was all there was to it.

Shelley turned around to speak to Hartley, because she had to confide in someone and she was sure he would understand.

"Shelley, is something wrong?" he asked, when he saw her face.

"Mr. Ericson gave me a D in biology," she said.

"I can't understand it. I've never had a D in my life."

Hartley's expression showed genuine concern. "Maybe there is a mistake someplace. Why don't you go talk to him?"

Yes, there must be a mistake someplace. There had to be. "Maybe he accidentally wrote someone else's grade on my card," Shelley said to Hartley. "You are right. I'll go talk to him."

"Good luck," said Hartley.

It was nice to know a boy who understood that grades were important. As Shelley walked toward the biology laboratory she began to have some misgivings. There had been that C on her first report card, but she had not been too worried about it because it was not a semester grade. And maybe her drawings of some of the things they had examined through a microscope weren't exactly works of art, but they weren't supposed to be, were they? This was biology, not art. And there was the time she had forgotten to draw the nucleus in the pleurococcus—that was the day Philip had asked her to go to the barn dance and naturally she had a lot of distracting things to think about. But a D! Shelley Latham did not get D's.

Shelley entered the biology room, where she pretended to look at some exhibits until the room was clear of students and she could speak to Mr. Ericson alone. "Mr. Ericson," she said tentatively as she approached his desk, where he was busy with some papers.

"Yes, Shelley," he said, looking up from his work.

"I think there might be a mistake on my report card," Shelley said nervously, because she was always ill at ease with Mr. Ericson. "I—I have a D in biology."

"There is no mistake," answered Mr. Ericson. "You earned that D fair and square."

Shelley felt her face turn red. "But I've never had a D in my life," she protested.

Mr. Ericson leaned back in his chair and smiled sardonically. "You have now."

"But Mr. Ericson," said Shelley desperately. "I want to go to college—"

"Why?" interrupted Mr. Ericson.

Shelley paused. Why did she want to go to college? No one had ever asked her this question before and she felt confused. She could not tell this man she wanted to go to college because all the girls she knew were planning to go or because her parents had told her she should go. Those were not the real reasons. "Because I want to have a career," she said lamely, although this was not the right answer.

"Oh, you do," said Mr. Ericson. "What sort of career?"

"I—I don't know. I mean, I haven't made up my mind yet." Shelley felt more and more uncomfortable with Mr. Ericson looking at her as if he expected her to explain herself concisely in outline form on a moment's notice. She decided to try changing the subject. "To go to college I have to maintain a B average," she said. "I just can't get D's."

"Then I would suggest that you stop doing D work," said Mr. Ericson.

Shelley found that there was not one thing that she could say. She was filled with anger and humiliation.

"Perhaps the seating arrangement for the semester was unfortunate," said Mr. Ericson.

Shelley looked sharply at her biology teacher. Was he referring to Philip? The gleam of amusement in his keen blue eyes told her that he was. "The seating arrangement had nothing to do with it," she said, with all the haughtiness she could manage.

"You know, I would not be doing you a favor if I gave you a B for D work in high school," Mr. Ericson said. "You will have to take a laboratory science in college, too, and if you do poor work, it is better to find out about it now while there is still time to do something about it than to wait until you are in college."

Probably this was true, but the way Shelley felt toward Mr. Ericson, she did not want to admit that anything he said was right. D—and this was only the first semester. She had months ahead of her of drawing crawly things under a microscope and dissecting the worm and the frog and the crayfish that came in the second semester. And all under the sardonic eye of Mr. Ericson, because in a school of this size there was only one biology teacher. Now she wouldn't dare even look at Philip during the whole eighty minutes of the period.

"I'll make a bargain with you," said Mr. Ericson. "If you turn in B work the second semester, I'll give you a C for the whole year."

"I'll do B work," promised Shelley and thought, If it kills me.

"Good," said Mr. Ericson, as if the subject were closed.

"Thank you, Mr. Ericson," Shelley said stiffly, and left the room. *Oh*, she thought as she left the building, that man! Who did he think he was, anyway? As if Philip had anything to do with this. Well, she would show him!

But gradually, as she walked down the road, Shelley's explosive mood spent itself. She felt ashamed because she had done poor work and embarrassed because Mr. Ericson had noticed her preoccupation with Philip. New feelings began to replace her anger.

The trouble with me, Shelley thought, is that I don't really have any brains. In elementary school she had kept her handwriting neat, her papers unsmudged, and her two-finger margins straight, so her teachers approved of her and gave her good grades. In high school, too, she was neat, prompt, and conscientious and so her teachers liked her. But brains, no. Giving good grades to Shelley Latham was just a habit with her teachers at home. Probably she didn't deserve them at all. But even while she railed at herself, Shelley knew that what she was telling herself was not true. Being conscientious had helped, of course, but she had always been a good student and had enjoyed most of her studies. Even in the subjects she had not enjoyed, her pride had kept her near the top of the class. That this was her first experience with a laboratory science was no excuse. Perhaps if Philip had not sat beside her . . .

Shelley turned into the opening in the privet hedge. And the worst of it was, Tom or Mavis would have to sign her report card and know about the D. It seemed as if there was to be no end to her humiliation. If only she hadn't taken biology. Maybe chemistry would have been better. But then Philip would not have been in her class and she might not have known him. Besides, chemistry smelled so awful. Now, knowing that Mr. Ericson's eagle eye was upon her, she wouldn't dare look at Philip. Old Eagle Eye Ericson. She had promised him B work and now she would have to study like a fiend at a subject she hated. She thought she hated it, but actually until today she had not thought much about the subject one way or another. She had been too busy thinking about Philip.

Shelley entered the house, tossed her books on a couch in the living room, and flopped down beside them. She sat brooding about the D. Dear Mother and Daddy, she would have to write. Today was report-card day and I was unpleasantly surprised to get a D in biology. I thought I had studied. . . .

Before Shelley could compose the letter, Katie burst through the front door. At first glance Shelley was shocked at the sight of her, and then she saw that Katie was smeared with lipstick. There were daubs of lipstick on her arms, smears of lipstick on her cheeks, and smudges of lipstick on her blouse, but her expression was radiant.

"Katie!" exclaimed Shelley. "What happened to you?"

Katie dropped into an armchair. "Well," she began, "Pamela and I were walking home from school. We were walking along just minding our own business and not doing a *thing*, when Pamela took a lipstick out of her purse to show me. It's a new shade called Lucky in Love and I think it's yummy. I don't see why Mommy won't let me wear lipstick for dress-up. She never lets me do *anything*. Anyway, Joe and Rudy came along and they asked Pamela if they could see her lipstick. Pamela gave it to them, never dreaming what they were going to do." Katie paused for breath. "And do you know what those crazy boys did?"

"I can guess," said Shelley.

"They started smearing us with lipstick," Katie continued with relish. "It was simply *awful*. They got lipstick all over us. And then I grabbed it away from Rudy and rubbed it all over his face." Katie sat smiling at this happy memory before she said regretfully, "I guess I better go wash it off before Mommy sees me. You know how she is."

Shelley recalled her own thirteen-year-old adventures walking home from school—the rain hat grabbed and thrown up into a tree, the scarf snatched and tied around the neck of a passing dog. "You like Rudy, don't you?" asked Shelley.

"Yes," admitted Katie frankly. "I have a terrible crush on him."

"What's he like?"

"Simply divine," said Katie, getting up to admire her smudges in the hall mirror. "Taller than I am, if you count the way his hair sort of sticks up." She started up the stairs. "Promise not to tell what I said about Rudy."

"I promise." After this interruption Shelley felt more cheerful. Watching Katie go through a phase she herself had outgrown always made Shelley feel serene and experienced, capable of meeting any situation that might arise in the course of growing up. She picked up her books and went to her room, where she looked through the second half of her biology book to see what lay ahead of her during the second semester.

When Shelley came downstairs sometime later she found Tom studying Luke's report cards while Luke, his face smudged with grease from his motorcycle, sat staring moodily out the window. "Luke, this doesn't make sense," Tom was saying. "An A in Latin and a C minus in English."

Luke was silent.

"You must have some explanation." Tom waited expectantly. "I am glad you earned an A in Latin, but how do you explain your grade in English?"

Luke looked unhappy. "Aw, Dad, you know how English is. All that stuff about sentence structure and having to read *Idylls of the King*."

"Sentence structure!" exclaimed Tom. "You complain about sentence structure in English and then get an A in Latin, which is much more complicated. Ablative absolute and *hic, haec, hoc*—Latin is much more difficult."

"Aw, Dad, don't you understand?" Luke asked. "I *like* my Latin teacher."

Shelley sympathized with Luke's problem. The next semester would be so much easier if she liked Mr. Ericson. Postponing the moment when she must confess her D, Shelley went into the dining room to set the table while Mavis prepared supper. When Tom finished discussing Luke's report card, he went into the kitchen and helped himself to an olive that Mavis was about to stir into a tamale pie.

Katie came thumping down the stairs and appeared in the kitchen. Her face was rosy from its recent scrubbing. "Dad, do you know what?" she asked, with an air of suppressed excitement. "Pamela said her father said if we divided up our orange grove and this property into lots and sold them we would be *rich.*"

"Oh, he did," answered Tom dry. "And what would we do with our riches?"

"Pamela says we could build a new house," said Katie. "A ranch house."

Oh, no, thought Shelley, forgetting her own problem for the moment. Not give up this comfortable, creaky old house and live in a house just like anyone else's.

"For the information of Pamela and her father, not that it is any of their business," began Tom, "it just so happens that I don't want to live in a new house. I like this house just as it is, slanting floors, too many doors, creaking stairs, and all. I like having my own trees around me, and room for the dog to run, and a place for your mother's studio, and extra bedrooms for Shelley and your grandmother and anyone else we want to visit us."

"Yes, that is nice," agreed Katie, and added wistfully, "but Pamela's house has wall-to-wall carpeting and all the furniture is Early American."

"Goodness!" exclaimed Mavis. "I wouldn't have wall-to-wall carpeting. I don't like to run the vacuum cleaner that much. And we have some Early American furniture. The secretary and those two little tables in the living room came from your grandmother's family home in New England and are very, very old."

"Oh, Mommy," said Katie impatiently. "I don't mean that kind of Early American. I mean *new* Early American like you buy in a store."

Mavis began to laugh. "Katie, you funny little girl. I think you see too much of Pamela."

Katie was injured. "I am not a funny little girl," she said, with her most dignified air. "I don't know why you always have to say things like that. Or why you have to criticize my friends all the time. Pamela is—"

"Katie," said Tom sternly. "You aren't by any chance trying to avoid the subject of report cards?"

Katie's dignity wilted. "Oh, all right," she said. "I got a C in cooking. But it really wasn't my fault at all. The teacher just doesn't like me. She picks on me."

"Poor kid," said Tom jovially.

"Daddy, do you always have to make fun of me?" asked Katie.

Tom ignored her question. "Perhaps you would do better in cooking if you had a little more practice at home."

"I do cook at home," said Katie. "I baked a cake yesterday."

"I mean cook from the basic raw materials, not

from a mix in a package," said Tom. "How about cooking some of the things you cook at school?"

"You mean like white sauce and mush?" asked Katie, and made a gagging noise.

"I'm game," said Tom. "Anything to raise your grade in cooking."

Shelley decided this was the time to speak. "I guess this must be the season for poor grades," she said with a nervous laugh. "I got a D in biology, but Mr. Ericson says if I get a B the second semester he will give me a C for the whole year."

"You see, Daddy?" Katie sounded triumphant. "I'm not the only one."

"Oh, Shelley, what a shame," said Mavis sympathetically. "But I am sure that if you apply yourself you won't have any trouble raising the grade. After all, with a subject like biology, all you really have to do is go to work and learn it."

Why, that's so, thought Shelley. She had never thought of it that way. She made up her mind that she would do exactly that—go to work and learn it.

"A D is worse than a C," observed Katie virtuously.

Shelley made a face at her. "But it isn't going to stay a D," she reminded Katie.

"That reminds me," remarked Tom, picking another olive out of the tamale pie.

"Tom!" objected Mavis. "There won't be any olives left if you keep this up."

"This is the last one," promised Tom. "I was just going to say that I lost a star basketball player today."

"What happened?" asked Mavis.

"Phil Blanton flunked biology," said Tom. "His father had told him that if he didn't keep his grades up he couldn't play basketball and so—no more basketball for Phil."

Shelley felt her face turn scarlet.

"He sits beside Shelley in biology," Katie lost no time in pointing out.

There was nothing Shelley could say. She looked into a cupboard so that she could turn her back to Tom and Mavis. Memories of biology came rushing back to her—the day Mr. Ericson stopped lecturing until she and Philip stopped whispering. The day they had made the date for the barn dance. Her D was bad enough, but an F! An F was really something to be ashamed of. And now Philip not only could not play on the team, the whole school would know he had flunked biology. The whole school already knew that she sat at the same table with him and everyone would blame her because he had flunked. The star of the team! The forward Tom had been counting on. All that was bad enough, but an F on Philip's record was far worse, because it might keep him from getting into college. Maybe she had ruined his whole career, even his whole life.

Shelley wondered what Philip would think of her now. If they had not been so aware of one another in class, if they had both worked harder . . . Then Shelley remembered that Philip had not asked to see her this week end.

Chapter 9

Friday evening Shelley tried to forget Philip while she dutifully studied biology. Because the new semester did not begin until Monday, she was studying when she did not actually have an assignment. She wished Mr. Ericson could see her now, her head bent over her textbook, and on Friday night, too. She could not forget Philip, however, and he occupied her thoughts while her eyes slid over the sentences in the biology book.

Time dragged on Saturday morning and Shelley made it drag even more by dawdling over the breakfast dishes. She wondered what Philip was doing. Perhaps he was out working someplace and thinking bitter thoughts about her, the girl who had caused him to flunk. She began to dread Monday and the moment when they would inevitably meet in the hall at school. Maybe he would look at her and glance away as if he did not even know her. Everyone would talk about them over sandwiches at noon. And with the basketball season about to start, too. She could never face going to the games and having the whole student body whisper and point her out as the girl who made the star forward flunk off the team.

Shelley swished her hands back and forth in the dishwater to stir up more suds. She dreaded seeing Philip but at the same time she longed to see him.

If she could only tell him how sorry she was and tell him about her D, he would understand.

Katie entered the kitchen and said enthusiastically, "I just saw an idea for a cute cake in a magazine."

In spite of her preoccupation with Philip, Shelley managed to laugh.

"Well, it *is* a cute cake. You take a package of cake mix"—Katie found a package in the cupboard—"and you bake it in two oblong pans. Then you cut one half in two the long way to make rabbit ears, and you frost the whole thing and sprinkle it with coconut and use jelly beans for the eyes and nose, and when you get through you have a cake that looks like a rabbit." Katie dumped the mix into a bowl, found two eggs in the refrigerator, carefully separated them and added the yolks to the mix along with the milk. The whites of the eggs she poured into the cat's dish. "Here, kitty, kitty," she called, and Smoky came running to lick up the egg. "I'll hide part of the cake from Luke so you and Philip can have some when he comes over tonight."

"Thank you, Katie," said Shelley, "but Philip isn't coming over tonight."

"Why?" demanded Katie, looking up from the batter she was about to beat.

"He just isn't," answered Shelley, running more hot water into the dishwater.

"Did you have a quarrel?" asked Katie, her eyes alight at this interesting possibility. "Did you tell him you never wanted to see him again?"

"No. Nothing like that." Shelley was hard pressed for an explanation. "He—well, he has something else to do." That was true enough, and she hoped the answer would satisfy Katie's curiosity for the time being.

Katie was busy reading the directions on the cake-mix box. "Wouldn't you know?" she exclaimed. "I needed those egg whites for the frosting." She took two more eggs out of the refrigerator, separated them, and gave the yolks to the cat. "Don't tell Daddy," she said. "You know how he is about wasting food." She beat her cake batter, counting under her breath, and when she finished, she said, "Pamela thinks Philip is the handsomest boy in school. I think so, too, but I thought Hartley was sort of nice that night he helped with the ironing."

"He is nice," said Shelley, as she emptied the dishpan. "I see him a lot at school, but—well, it is just different with Philip." The ringing of the telephone startled Shelley so she dropped the dishcloth. Sometimes the ring of a telephone could be such a hopeful sound.

Katie set down her bowl and went into the dining room to answer. "Yes, just a minute," she said. "It's for you, Shelley."

Shelley caught her breath. Philip? Her eyes must have asked the question.

"I think it's that big old Frisbie," whispered Katie.

Oh. Frisbie. Why should he telephone her? Shelley hoped he did not think that just because Philip was through with her that he could ask her for a date. After all, he was Philip's best friend. Shelley picked up the telephone but did not answer at once. She was looking at the San Sebastian telephone book. It was a mere pamphlet compared to the telephone book at home. "Hello?" she said in an impersonal voice.

"Hello, Shelley," said Philip.

"Philip!" Shelley's heart beat fast. "I thought—"

"I had Friz make the call because I didn't know who would answer and I didn't feel like talking to the coach," Philip explained. "Look, Friz and I have a job splitting some eucalyptus wood down the road from the Michies' and I wondered if you could come by. I—I want to talk to you."

"Why—" Shelley hesitated, trying to think. Maybe she should insist on his coming to the house. Still, he did have a job to do and she could understand how he might not want to talk to Tom right now. "All right," she agreed happily, because Philip did not sound angry or even bitter. He sounded anxious. Perhaps he thought she would think he was blaming her for his F and wanted her to know he didn't feel that way at all. Whatever it was he wanted to talk about, everything was going to be all right.

"You know the place," said Philip. "Where I told you we took down the tree last week."

"Yes, I'll be there in a little while," answered Shelley. Philip was not angry with her. He wanted to see her right away. He couldn't even wait until this evening.

"Katie, be an angel and dry the dishes," said Shelley, when she had replaced the receiver.

"Sure," said Katie. "Are you going out with Frisbie?"

"No, with Philip." Shelley could not keep the lilt out of her voice. She ran up to her room to comb her hair and then left by the front door to avoid any more questions from Katie. She hurried down the road, following the sound of metal ringing against metal, until she saw Philip and Frisbie. Then she walked more slowly so she would not appear too eager.

When Philip saw her he leaned his maul against a section of a eucalyptus tree, dropped his wedges on the ground, and came to meet her. They stood facing one another under the arching fronds of a low palm tree beside some neglected-looking geraniums. Philip's face was dirty and he wiped the sweat from his forehead with the sleeve of his sweat shirt.

"Hi," he said, looking serious. "I suppose you heard I can't play basketball because I flunked biology?"

"Well—yes, I did," Shelley admitted. "I feel awful about it. As if it were partly my fault."

"Aw, Shelley, don't feel that way," pleaded Philip. "It wasn't your fault."

"I—I got a D," Shelley confessed reluctantly.

"Did you?" remarked Philip. "Well, that's better than flunking."

Shelley was surprised that he did not show more concern. Of course a D was better than an F, but it still was nothing to be so casual about. "But now I can't be on the honor roll," she said.

"I wouldn't know. I've never been on it," was Philip's offhand answer. He picked up a eucalyptus bud that lay in the road and pegged it at a telephone pole. "I'll miss playing on the team," he remarked.

"I know," said Shelley sympathetically, "but what about college? Will this keep you from getting in?"

"Maybe," answered Philip, pegging another eucalyptus bud at an orange tree. "But I don't care."

"Don't care!" Shelley was shocked. "You mean you don't care whether or not you go to college?"

"I don't even want to go," answered Philip.

"You don't want to go to college?" Shelley could scarcely believe it. It was true that she could not explain to Mr. Ericson why she wanted to go to college, but at the same time she was sure college was important. "But I thought everyone wanted to go to college."

"I don't," answered Philip. "Everyone wants me to go—Mom and Dad think just because they went to the university I should go, too, but I don't want to go. They're pretty disappointed in me, I guess, and I feel awful about it because they are really swell."

"But—why don't you want to go to college?" asked Shelley.

"Because I don't like to study," answered Philip. "I feel all cooped up sitting at a desk with a pile of books. I like to be outdoors doing things—things like cutting trees. Dad wants me to be a lawyer or something and I'm not cut out for it."

"But you can't cut trees all your life," Shelley protested.

"Why can't I?" asked Philip. "Lots of men earn their livings cutting trees and clearing land, especially now that there is so much building going on. Of course I'm not sure that's what I want to do, but it is one thing I could do."

Shelley was silent. She broke off a sprig of geranium still damp from yesterday's rain and carefully pulled the dead blossoms from the cluster. Philip earning his living cutting trees—this did not fit in with her picture of him at all. The fairy-tale phrase, "poor woodcutter," popped into her mind. How silly, she thought. Nobody was a poor woodcutter in this day and age. She felt sorry for Philip. It must be hard for a boy to study when he disliked studying. And he was going to miss so much.

"If it weren't for the team and Dad's feeling so bad, I wouldn't even care about flunking," said Philip moodily. "That and one other thing."

"What is that?" asked Shelley.

Philip picked up another eucalyptus bud and took careful aim at a dove on a telephone wire. He missed but the dove flew away. "Shelley—I feel terrible about this," he said, looking down at her. "Dad says I can't have any more dates until I bring my grades up."

Shelley stared at Philip, not quite believing what

he said. Then, embarrassed, she began to pluck the fresh petals from the geranium one by one. He loves me, he loves me not. He loves me, he loves me not. She could not keep the words from running through her mind.

"Dad is pretty strict," explained Philip. "That's why I couldn't often ask you for a date ahead of time. If he thought I hadn't studied enough during the week, he wouldn't let me go out on week ends."

So Philip had not been so casual after all. And now she was being given notice. Shelley did not know what to say. What could she say—thanks, it's been nice knowing you and now I'll run along? And what would her mother think when she found a boy was not allowed to go out with her?

"I'm sure sorry, Shelley," said Philip. "I feel terrible about it."

"I—I guess you can't help it." Shelley's fingers continued to pluck at the geranium. He loves me, he loves me not. One more petal. He loves me. She threw the empty stem to the ground.

"You're not angry?" Philip sounded anxious.

"No, I'm not angry," answered Shelley. What was there to be angry about?

"Swell," said Philip. "I knew you'd understand. I'll really work to bring my grades up."

"You do that, Philip." Shelley found she felt completely blank, as if she did not have any emotions. "Well, I guess I'd better go now."

Suddenly Philip took her hand. "You're awfully nice, Shelley."

Shelley smiled faintly. "Thank you, Philip. Good luck. I'll miss you in class next semester."

"Oh, I'll be there," said Philip. "They are letting me take the second semester and then I have to repeat the first semester next year."

"Oh," was all Shelley said. This was worse. To sit beside Philip another semester when he could not come to see her and the whole school would know about it. . . . Feeling as if she were walking in her sleep, Shelley turned and left. She walked slowly past the grove and through the privet hedge and into the house. She climbed the creaking stairs and sat down on her unhemmed bedspread. She felt numb, but beneath the numbness was hurt pride. It hurt to have a boy tell her he was not allowed to go out with her. And it was going to hurt even more to have the whole school know she wanted to go out with him when he was not allowed to go out with her. And then there were the letters filled with references to Philip that she had written to her mother and to Rosemary. It had been such a joy to write his name.

Shelley sat listening to the whir of a lawn mower down the road. Now there was no longer any reason to write Philip's name at all. He was not allowed to go out with her and there was nothing she could do about it. San Sebastian was not a magic place. She could not perform some task that would break a magic spell and free him. And his father was not an ogre. He was a man who wanted his son to do well in school.

Shelley felt sorry for Philip. It would almost be easier if he were the kind of boy who would rebel, but he wasn't. He would do the best he could in that reserved way of his, trying to please his father and knowing in the long run he wouldn't. It must be hard for him to study when he didn't like studying. She was sorry, too, because he did not want to go to college. There was no reason why everyone should go to college, but for herself, she knew that her life would be more interesting if she did go. That was what she should have told Mr. Ericson. But Philip was not the kind of boy who wanted to go. . . .

Shelley buried her face in her bedspread. She was suddenly and desperately homesick. She was homesick for her mother and father and for Rosemary. She was homesick for the soft Oregon rain and the feel of dampness against her cheeks when she walked home from school. She was homesick for definite seasons, autumn leaves in fall and iris and violets that understood they should bloom when spring had come. She was homesick for fir trees in the park and sea gulls wheeling over the school lawn when there was a storm at sea. She was homesick for the mahogany dining-room table and fluffy pink bath towels. She was homesick for those drinking fountains that were never turned off.

Outside, the eucalyptus leaves rustled in the breeze and from down the road the sound of the lawn mower continued. There was something wrong about that sound and at first Shelley could not think what it was. Then she knew. It was a lawn mower in winter. At home the sound of the first lawn mower meant that spring had come, even though no one wrote poetry about it. Now Shelley listened to the lawn mower and thought about the four long months that were still ahead of her in this strange country. From now until the first week in June. She did not know how she could face them without Philip.

Chapter 10

In her homesickness Shelley saw San Sebastian through different eyes. The tan stucco high school with its imitation mission tower seemed ugly when compared to her red-brick school at home. And palm trees— how could she ever have thought those trees with their ragged dirty petticoats of dead fronds were exciting to behold? She began to recall the little things she had missed in California, really crisp eating apples and the cozy feeling of being in a warm bed when sleet was slatting against the windows.

Even enrolling in Journalism 1, a class Shelley had looked forward to since she started high school, did not help. She found the subject interesting and she enjoyed being in the same class with Hartley, but her enthusiasm was gone. Biology lab was every bit as difficult as she had expected it to be. She felt humiliated. The other members of the class exchanged knowing glances, the way she had known they would. She appreciated Jeannie's silent sympathy, but she found being in a situation that called for sympathy hard to take. Frisbie's knowing smile was downright irritating.

But Philip—it was the presence of Philip himself that was hardest to bear. He still talked to her in his shy and courteous way but there was a difference now, as if he, too, knew that things could never be the same. The sight of him working so doggedly over his dissecting pan and notebook was painful to Shelley. What kind of person was she, anyhow, to grind up roses at home and then come down here and cause Philip so much unhappiness? When the class came to the worm-dissecting assignment, Shelley asked herself what was the one thing in the world she least wanted to do. The answer was easy. Cutting up a worm in San Sebastian, California, under the sharp eyes of Mr. Ericson beside a boy who was not allowed to go out with her.

Shelley mentioned Oregon so often that Frisbie said, "If you like it up there so much, why don't you go back?" And once when Shelley started to say, "In Oregon we always—" someone interrupted by saying, "We will now pause while Shelley delivers a commercial." After that Shelley was miserable in silence. She couldn't go back now. At home the second semester was well under way and she would be behind in her classes if she transferred now. Besides, her father had told her that if she came to California, he expected her to stay for the whole school year.

The weather grew colder. Snow fell in the mountains, and the sight of the green trees loaded with golden oranges against a background of snow-topped mountains almost raised Shelley's spirits. Then she found that San Sebastian paid a price for this beauty.

At eight o'clock in the evening the Michies turned on the radio to listen anxiously to the frost warnings. Tom went out in the night to check the temperature in the grove. Later he called Luke out of bed to help light the smudge pots. Shelley was awakened by the smell of oily smoke and a sound like the roar of airplane propellers. When she got up to close her bedroom window she saw flames shooting up from the smudge pots throughout the groves and knew that the wind machines were fanning heated air through the trees. It was an eerie and beautiful sight, like nothing Shelley had ever seen before. These Californians, who thought they could heat up all out of doors! What was she doing here, anyway?

In the morning Tom and Luke came in red-eyed, washed but not clean. They had stopped to try to scrub off the greasy smoke in the showers at the gym, but smudge did not wash off easily. Their eyes were rimmed with black, and when Shelley went to school she saw that many of the boys had the same washed-but-not-clean look. As the day wore on, heads began to nod over books and drop down on folded arms. Shelley noticed Mr. Ericson smiling sympathetically at Frisbie sleeping in biology lab. She had not known her teacher was that human.

The next days were anxious ones. Tom and Luke were grimy and tired. Mavis was worried. "We have a tiger by the tail," she told Shelley. "Once we start smudging we can't stop until the cold spell breaks. If it should be a long one it can eat up all the profit from the oranges."

The smudging continued for three nights before the temperature rose and the Michie household returned to normal. Shelley then felt it worthwhile to wash the smudge out of her hair. She had never been inconvenienced by a crop before. Things like that did not happen in the city, thank goodness.

One day while Shelley was trying to make herself eat a sandwich, Jeannie suddenly asked, "You are really in love with him, aren't you?"

"In love?" repeated Shelley, surprised. Love was such a big word, almost too big to talk about. "Why, I suppose . . . I always think of love as something that comes later."

Jeannie did not say anything. She just looked at

Shelley with her sharp, bright eyes. A few days later she said, "Let's go to the basketball game together."

Shelley had been dreading the basketball season. "Well . . . no, Jeannie," she answered vaguely. "You'd better not count on me. I doubt if I can make it."

"If you say so." Jeannie's glance was sharp and penetrating.

Shelley was so homesick she even wrote to Jack, whose last unanswered letter had lain on her desk for over two months. Her letter was short—she was really not eager to communicate with Jack. It was just that he was someone at home. Letters to her mother were more difficult. In each one she carefully managed to include some reference to Philip so that her mother would not wonder what had happened to him and start asking awkward questions that might force Shelley to confess that Philip was not allowed to take her out.

Then came the night of the first basketball game with Santa Theresa, the night Philip could not play. Shelley had made up her mind that she could not face this game. She had to go to school but she did not have to attend a basketball game. She felt so miserable she thought perhaps she was coming down with a cold.

Tom left the house early that evening. Shelley went up to her room to study. Her head felt heavy and when she swallowed, she was pretty sure her throat was scratchy or was going to be. She heard some of Luke's friends stop for him on the way to the game. Soon Mavis and Katie would be gone and she would have the whole house to herself. She was so miserable she felt as if in complete solitude she would dissolve into a puddle of tears.

Shelley sat huddled at her desk when Katie knocked and entered. "Hi," said Shelley forlornly. She knew that Katie would not mention Philip, because she had not spoken his name since the day he told Shelley he could not see her. This was so unlike Katie that Shelley was sure Mavis had taken her aside and told her to say nothing about Philip.

"Come on, go to the game with Mommy and me," Katie pleaded.

"No, thanks, Katie," said Shelley with a wan smile. "I really don't feel like it."

Mavis appeared in the doorway behind Katie. "Come on, Shelley," she urged.

Shelley smiled and shook her head.

"It will be lots more fun if you come," begged Katie.

Shelley was touched as she always was by Katie's eagerness for her company, but she still shook her head.

"Come on, Shelley. You'll feel better if you go." There was quiet insistence in Mavis's voice.

Shelley was, after all, a guest in the Michies' house and Mavis was the coach's wife. Shelley had an obligation to please whether she felt like it or not. "All right," she agreed, trying to conceal her reluctance as she pulled her coat out of the closet.

The gymnasium where the two teams were already warming up was bedlam. Pairs of yell leaders from both schools were leading yells that seemed to Shelley to reverberate from the walls and ceiling. Santa Theresa had brought along an electric megaphone that added to the din.

Mavis led the way to the section of seats across the aisle from the coach's bench, where room was soon found for the family of the popular coach. "Thank goodness, San Sebastian is expected to win," she remarked, as they sat down on the bench.

Shelley supposed she should have worn a white

blouse and sat in the rooting section behind the team, but she was too dispirited to care. She did not feel like mingling with the other students and wondering what they were thinking of her.

The referee blew his whistle and tossed the ball into the air to start the game. It was at that moment that Shelley saw Philip, sitting on the end of the players' bench farthest from her. He was wearing his letter man's sweater, the sweater that would not have a second strip added to the sleeve at the end of the year. His feet were spread apart, his hands were in his pockets, and he was leaning forward, tense, following the ball as if he were playing the game himself. Shelley was surprised to see him, although she realized she should not have been. A boy like Philip would care about the game even though he was not allowed to play.

San Sebastian scored. Santa Theresa scored through the basket at the end of the gym where Shelley and Philip had scattered hay a long time ago. "Take it away! Take it away!" chanted the San Sebastian rooting section. "Score! Score!" yelled the opposing section, the rooters making their voices swoop up on each word. The leader with the electric megaphone was carried away by the sound of his own voice electrically magnified until it seemed to Shelley to fill the entire gymnasium with sound waves so vibrant they were almost visible.

San Sebastian scored twice. Philip could not sit still on the bench and when he sprang up for a better view, Shelley wished desperately for her school to win to make up for Philip's not being allowed to play. Katie jumped up and down and screamed. Santa Theresa made three baskets in a row. A San Sebastian player fell and hurt his knee. Time out. Philip sat down on the bench sideways, facing the player beside him, talking earnestly.

The playing started again. The referee's whistle shrilled. There was a foul against Santa Theresa. "Score! Score!" swooped the electrically led rooting section. "Take it away! Take it away!" screamed San Sebastian. Santa Theresa scored. The ball was in the hands of a San Sebastian player, who was dribbling it down the length of the gym. Philip was on his feet again. The ball teetered maddeningly on the edge of the basket, wobbled, and fell through. The electric megaphone seemed to be ringing inside Shelley's head. Katie beat her arm in excitement. More shouts, more feet pounding on the floor, more arms waving, the referee's whistle and, somehow, Santa Theresa was ahead by four points at the half.

Girl yell leaders took over the floor with their giant pompons of colored crepe paper, green and yellow for San Sebastian, purple and white for Santa Theresa. They performed their stylized dances, shaking their pompons to the right and to the left while Philip sat with his hands clasped between his knees.

"I do so hope Tom wins his first game," said Mavis, "but now I am not so sure."

"He's got to win," said Katie.

The pompon girls left the floor and the janitor came out with a push broom to sweep up the scraps of crepe paper left behind. This time, when play was resumed, San Sebastian was trying for the basket through which Philip had shot an imaginary ball when he and Shelley were decorating for the barn dance. That bittersweet memory. San Sebastian scored three times in succession and the rooting section was in a frenzy. Then suddenly in front of Shelley there was a tangle of sinewy legs and sweating bodies. She and Katie had to throw up their arms in front of their faces to avoid being struck by the ball.

Shelley knew then that Philip must have seen her, and after that she would not let herself look in his direction. She wondered what he was thinking about her, if indeed he bothered to think about her at all. It would be so much easier if they had quarreled or he had met a girl he liked better or she had met another boy. Then she would have had some idea of how to behave, because she knew how other girls had acted (and perhaps should not have acted) in those more ordinary situations.

The rest of the game for Shelley was a noisy blur of knees, elbows, and a bouncing, flying ball. And then it was over and San Sebastian had lost. Mavis was quiet. Katie drooped. Shelley had a glimpse of Philip talking to one of the players on his way to the locker room. He looked serious and from the gestures he was making with his hands, he seemed to be re-enacting one of the plays.

And it was all Shelley's fault. Things might have been different if Philip could have played. Now all she wanted to do was to leave the gymnasium without meeting him. This should not be hard to do. Philip, she was sure, would not want to meet her.

Shelley followed Mavis and Katie through the straggling crowd that had cheered for the losing team. At the end of the gym, under the basket that San Sebastian's ball had too often failed to go through, Shelley felt a hand on her shoulder. It was a boy's hand, and the feel of it made her start. She looked back and found herself looking into Hartley's dark eyes.

Hartley smiled at her, a sympathetic smile. "Don't feel that way," he said. "It's only a game, you know."

"I know, but—" was all Shelley could say.

"I know," answered Hartley, and Shelley knew that he did know. He patted her shoulder and with an encouraging smile, disappeared into the crowd.

Shelley found she felt a little better. Somehow, Hartley's pat on the shoulder had helped, because it showed he understood how she felt. She thought of the evening he had helped with the Michies' ironing and had taken her to Vincente. She had really enjoyed that evening, but of course that was a long time ago.

Chapter 11

It was the mail that brought about a change in Shelley's feelings. On this particular delivery the mailman left in the Michie mailbox two letters for Shelley and a package for Katie. All three were to prove important to Shelley.

Shelley returned from school one afternoon to find Mavis reading a book with Smoky curled up in her lap and Sarge lying on the rug at her feet. "How did biology go today?" Mavis asked, looking up from her book.

"Ugh. We dissected a crayfish," answered Shelley and then added thoughtfully, "but you know, dissecting is rather interesting. A worm has five pairs of hearts. I didn't know that until I dissected one."

"There are a couple of letters for you," said Mavis.

Shelley knew. She had spotted them on the mantel the moment she entered the room. Never had mail seemed so precious, and the most precious letters of all came in the square white envelopes addressed in her mother's neat handwriting and the pale-blue envelopes that displayed the handwriting Rosemary was experimenting with this year, a backhand with little circles instead of dots over the *i*'s. Rosemary was always experimenting with something—nail polish, hair styles, personalities.

Now Shelley picked up the two letters, and as she

did so she noticed beside them the package addressed to Katie. Sitting on the couch she weighed the two letters on her finger tips before she decided to open Rosemary's first. It was written on notebook paper and many of the words were underlined.

"Dear Shelley," it began. "I'm writing in study period as usual—I have so much to do I'm simply *frantic*, to put it mildly. Anyway, you're sure lucky to be way down there in sunny California practically *surrounded* by handsome basketball players." (How am I ever going to explain Philip away, Shelley wondered. Of course she could not admit Philip was not allowed to go out with her, not after the way she had described him to Rosemary.) "Jack turns up once in a while to take me to the movies or something. But don't worry. We are Just Pals and I am keeping him safe from Other Women until you come back in case you still want him. I think he's sort of cute, though. Right after you left he took me to this movie that was made in Italy where everybody kept saying *a rivederci* (I guess that's how you spell it) instead of good-by and now Jack says it too. Don't worry—as I said before, we are Just Pals, but the way things are around here a boy in the hand is worth two in the bush or any old port in a storm or something like that. Anyway, it is beginning to snow here, not that a little snow would interest anyone who spends all her time lolling about under a palm tree—"

Shelley giggled and dropped the letter into her lap. If Rosemary could know what San Sebastian was like during smudging! Then Shelley picked up the letter and reread it thoughtfully. She had half hoped Rosemary would like Jack so much she would want to go steady with him. Apparently this was not going to happen. And now Jack was saying *a rivederci*. Well, as Rosemary said, probably a boy in the hand was worth two in the bush. Rosemary was always so practical about these things.

Shelley tore open her mother's letter, which had come by airmail, and, as always happened when she opened a letter from her mother, the guilty memory of the morning she threw the roses in the Disposall crossed her mind. "Shelley dear," the letter began. "I am so glad biology is going smoothly for you this semester. Philip sounds like a very nice boy and it must be pleasant to have him sitting beside you a second semester. Mavis writes that his family is very well liked in San Sebastian. I hope, dear, that you will remember that living in a small town is quite different from living in the city and that everyone will notice everything you do. I am sure Philip is a very nice boy and I know I can trust you not to lose your head—"

Shelley stopped reading. Lose her head! As if she had a chance! Honestly. I'll put it on my list, she thought. If I ever have a daughter my age I will not talk about her losing her head. And if her daughter went away to school, she would not write for references on every boy she happened to go out with. What did her mother think she was—a child? Shelley did considerable mental sputtering before she went on reading. "By the way, whatever happened to the boy named Hartley, whom you mentioned when you first went to California? It has begun to snow here and by tomorrow your father will probably have to shovel the driveway before he can get the car out. It seems only yesterday that I used to bundle you into your snow suit and red mittens so you could run out to catch the first snowflakes."

Shelley folded the letter and returned it to its envelope. Poor Mother, she thought, she really does miss me even if I was so awful about the raincoat that day. She sounded lonely. But even if she was lonely, Shelley wished she would not write to Mavis for references and talk about Shelley's losing her head.

Shelley looked across the room at Mavis and was grateful to her. Mavis had simply written a nice letter answering her old friend's inquiries about Philip and had said nothing about his not coming to see Shelley any more. She had not mentioned the matter to Shelley, either, although Shelley was sure she knew all about it, and for this Shelley was also grateful.

And the worst of it was, Shelley did not know how she was going to explain Philip away in her letters. She had mentioned him often and enthusiastically, because she knew her mother wanted her to have a good time. When she had reluctantly confessed her D she had not mentioned Philip at all, because she did not think her mother would approve of a boy who flunked. Shelley did not want to confess the real reason she was not going out with Philip. After all, she had her pride. Maybe she should start making casual references to other boys in her letters. Her mother had already inquired about Hartley. Now that he was in her journalism class, she saw him more often and it would be easy enough to say something about him in her letters home.

Katie came in through the front door and flung her books on a chair. "A package from Nana!" she exclaimed, when she saw the package on the mantel. "Loot!"

"Katie, what an expression!" said Mavis with a laugh. "What would your grandmother think if she could hear you?"

Eagerly Katie pulled the string off the package, threw the brown paper on the floor, and opened the box. Shelley saw the pleasure on her face fade to disappointment and then to dislike.

"What's the matter?" asked Mavis.

"It's a sweater," answered Katie in a flat voice.

"Just what you've been wanting," said Mavis. "Let's see it."

Katie held up the sweater briefly and then dropped it back into its box.

"Why, it's a lovely sweater," said Mavis.

Shelley agreed. The sweater was a delicate apricot color becoming to Katie. It was knit of soft yarn with a double row of cable stitch down the front. "You're certainly lucky," observed Shelley. "It's just right to wear with your brown skirt."

Katie looked obstinate.

"Katie, you're acting as if you don't like the sweater," said Mavis.

"I won't wear it!" Katie was so vehement that even Sarge lifted his nose from his paws to look at her.

"Katie!" exclaimed Mavis. "Of course you'll wear it."

"No, I won't," said Katie, "and nobody can make me!"

Inwardly Shelley was embarrassed. This all sounded much too familiar. She and her mother had said these same words so many times.

Mavis began to sound impatient. "Now why on earth should you refuse to wear a beautiful sweater like this?"

Katie stared at the floor. "It's hand-knit," she said finally. "With *cable* stitch." She made cable stitch sound like something peculiarly loathsome.

Mavis could not help laughing. "Katie, how ridiculous," she said. "That makes the sweater all the more lovely."

"I'm *not* ridiculous," said Katie resentfully. "I don't see why you have to go around saying I am ridiculous all the time."

Mavis ignored this outburst. "Katie, you couldn't go into a store and buy a sweater as lovely as this," she pointed out.

"I don't want to go into a store and buy a sweater like this," said Katie stubbornly.

Mavis's controlled patience reminded Shelley of her own mother. "But dear," said Mavis, "why don't you want to wear a hand-knit sweater?"

"Nobody wears hand-knit sweaters," said Katie. "The kids would make fun of me."

"No, they wouldn't," contradicted Mavis gently.

And they probably would, too, thought Shelley, remembering how her classmates had behaved about any unusual clothing when she was Katie's age. If they did not openly make fun of her, they would somehow make her feel as if there were something odd about her appearance.

"What kind of sweater would you prefer?" asked Mavis curiously.

"A plain old Orlon sweater from Penney's," said Katie emphatically. "The kind the rest of the kids wear."

"Oh, Katie!" Mavis's exclamation was a mixture of amusement, impatience, and irritation.

"Mother, you just don't understand," protested Katie.

"That seems to be a favorite phrase of yours," commented Mavis.

"Well, you *don't* understand," said Katie, "and I am *not* going to wear the sweater!"

"Of course you'll wear the sweater," said Mavis firmly. "You have been needing a sweater and now you have one, a very becoming one. And what is more, your grandmother is coming to visit us in a few weeks and I shall expect you to behave yourself."

"I'll freeze to death first." Katie thrust up her chin and stared out the window.

Shelley tried not to smile. She knew Katie was thinking, I'll freeze to death and then you'll be sorry.

"That would be pretty hard to do in San Sebastian," remarked Mavis drily.

"Oh, Mother!" Katie was angry. "Why do you always have to go and say things like that? Why can't you ever *understand?*"

"I don't know," said Mavis wearily. "But I do understand one thing. You are going to wear that sweater and no more nonsense. You know what your father would say."

Katie was silent as a variety of emotions passed over her face. Anger, stubbornness, the brink of tears. Finally she settled on haughtiness. "All right, I'll wear the old sweater," she said coldly, as she pulled it out of its box and jammed her arms into the sleeves. "Come on, Sarge, let's go."

The dog rose from the rug, shook himself, and trotted over to the door. Katie paused dramatically with her hand on the doorknob. "Why do *I* have to have a grandmother who knits?" she asked rhetorically before she flounced out, slamming the door behind her.

Poor Katie. Shelley's impulse was to run after her and say, It's all right about the sweater—really it is. All Katie needed was to feel that she was as attractive as Pamela, and to have Rudy dance with her at dancing class, and then it wouldn't matter what kind of sweater she wore. But it would not do any good to tell Katie this. She would not believe it until she found out for herself, just as Shelley had to learn about the raincoat for herself.

Mavis sank back into her chair with a sigh. "Well, I hope slamming the door makes her feel better."

"It probably does," said Shelley. "Where does her grandmother live?"

"Up in Carmel-by-the-sea," answered Mavis. "She has a little house that she lives in during the winter and rents out during the tourist season while she visits her children or travels. She expects to come down early this year, because she has it rented for the entire season to an elderly couple from the Valley who want to escape the heat."

The house was quiet without Katie clumping up and down the stairs. In the distance, through the grove, Sarge's barks could be heard. There seemed to be nothing for Shelley to add to the conversation. "Well, back to the salt mines," she remarked, and carried her books up to her room.

Shelley spent the rest of the afternoon reading the next chapter in her biology book, with frequent pauses when she propped her chin on her fist, stared out the window, and composed letters to her mother and to Rosemary. Dear Mother and Daddy, I can't imagine how I happened not to mention Hartley lately. Just a lapse of memory, I guess. He is in my journalism class and I see him all the time. More than I see Philip, really. . . . Dear Rosemary, Where on *earth* did you ever get the idea I was practically surrounded by basketball players? I may know one or two but I also know an interesting journalism student. I may have mentioned him before. His name is Hartley Lathrop and he . . .

And he what, Shelley asked herself. It was not going to be easy to give the impression that Hartley was important to her if she saw him only in the classroom. It would be a good idea, even fun, to see him outside the classroom, but she did not see how this could ever happen. If only she had explained her peculiar behavior the time he said good night to her, things might be different now.

Shelley stared out the window and turned over in her mind the one date she had shared with Hartley. From the garage came a feeble pop-pop-popping sound from Luke's motorcycle. Sarge's bark in the distance reminded Shelley of Katie, and as she listened she wondered what Katie was going to do about the sweater. She would not wear it to school. Shelley was sure of that. Not a girl like Katie.

It was almost suppertime before Katie appeared. She came through the back door into the kitchen, where Shelley was helping Mavis prepare the meal. "Mommy!" cried Katie. "Just look what happened."

The front of the sweater was covered with muddy streaks and a large raveled hole was torn in one side, revealing more muddy streaks on the white blouse she was wearing under the sweater.

"Katie, I'm surprised at you," said Mavis coldly.

"But Mommy," protested Katie with conspicuous innocence, "I couldn't help it. I was running along with Sarge in the grove and I picked up a stick for him to fetch and before I could throw it, he jumped up on me and tore my sweater. Honest, Mommy, it all happened so fast I didn't even know what was happening."

Shelley watched fascinated. Surely Mavis would not let Katie get away with this.

"Don't you believe me?" asked Katie, wide-eyed.

"No, I do not." Mavis dropped a lump of butter into a pan of peas. "Take your sweater off," she said mildly. "After supper you must write your grandmother a nice thank-you letter. And we won't be able to buy you a new sweater. We do not waste clothing in this household."

"Mommy," exclaimed Katie tragically, "I don't see why you don't believe me."

Mavis looked levelly at her daughter. "Supper is almost ready," she said.

After supper Katie went to her room without having to be told, and in half an hour she appeared with a sheet of note paper in her hand. "Is this all right, Mommy?" she asked.

Mavis took the letter and read it carefully. "Except that there are two *p*'s in *appreciate*, it is a very nice letter."

"O.K., I'll fix it," agreed Katie cheerfully.

"And when your grandmother comes to visit us perhaps she can reknit the part of the sweater that was torn," said Mavis.

Katie groaned, but it was a cheerful groan. She had worked something out of her system and as far as she was concerned, the incident was closed. She sat down on the couch and said softly, as she curled up beside her mother, "Mommy, tell me what it was like in the olden time when you were a little girl."

Mavis smiled down at her daughter and glanced toward Shelley, explaining in her glance that this was a family joke. "In the olden time when I was a little girl," she began, as if she were telling a story, "there were no nylon stockings or Kleenex. Ladies wore silk stockings and little girls learned to iron by practicing on linen handkerchiefs. And three times a week a truck came down the street bringing ice for the iceboxes in people's kitchens, and all the neighborhood children climbed onto the back of the truck to pick up bits of ice to suck. . . ."

Shelley smiled at Mavis and her daughter as she listened. So the argument about the sweater was all over. Neither had won. Mavis had not succeeded in making Katie wear a sweater she did not want to wear, and Katie would have to go without a new sweater which she needed. And yet somehow it made no difference in their feelings toward one another. Maybe that was the way it was with mothers and daughters. Nobody ever really won.

That sweater was to Katie as roses in the Disposall were to me, thought Shelley, stating the whole thing like an algebra problem. But this was a problem that could not be solved by algebra. That was the trouble with people—they didn't fit into formulas. Perhaps every girl had to throw roses into the Disposall at some time, because that was part of growing up. And suddenly Shelley knew that this was true. She did not understand why, but she knew that it was true.

Shelley knew then that she was not going to be haunted by those roses nearly so much, now that she knew she was not alone in her rebellious feelings. But she still had another problem to occupy her mind and she turned her thoughts to it now—how she was going to keep her mother from knowing why Philip did not come to see her any more. She would have to mention Philip less and less and write about Hartley more and more. . . . There must be some way she could make Hartley take an interest in her again. . . .

"And in the olden time when I was a little girl," Mavis continued, "cars did not have heaters or radios. Everyone carried an auto robe for people who rode in the back seat to put over their legs in winter. Some cars had little vases for flowers on the dashboard—"

"Flowers on the dashboard?" Katie murmured sleepily. "Mommy, you are just making it up."

Shelley was happier than she had been since the day she received her D in biology.

Chapter 12

At school Shelley set out to recapture Hartley's interest, not only to be able to write home about him, but because she missed the companionship of a boy. She managed to walk down the hall toward the journalism room a step ahead of him. Since they shared a common destination, Hartley naturally caught up with her.

"Oh, hello, Hartley," said Shelley, acting surprised to see him. "I liked that personal interview you wrote for class last week. It was different from what most of the class wrote."

"Thanks, Shelley." Hartley was pleased by her compliment. "I think a lot of interviews printed in the school paper are pretty silly. You know, the reporter always asks what was the subject's most embarrassing moment and who is his current heart interest. I thought I could make an interview with the janitor more interesting than that stuff."

"You did," Shelley assured him.

"By the way, have you decided what you are going to do for that informative interview assignment?" Hartley asked.

"Not yet," admitted Shelley, as they entered the journalism room. "Mrs. Boyce said it was all right to go to church and write up the sermon, but that doesn't seem like a real interview."

"I haven't thought of anything either," said Hartley. "I suppose I could interview my dad on the state of citriculture in California."

"But interviewing your father doesn't sound like a real interview either," said Shelley.

"I know," agreed Hartley, "but I haven't thought of anybody better."

"Me either," said Shelley, thinking that perhaps this was her chance. If she could think of a really good subject, she and Hartley might interview him together if she suggested it in the right way. But the subject would have to be interesting and unusual. Hartley was serious about journalism, as he was about all his subjects.

That evening Shelley was still trying to think of someone to interview as she picked up the *San Sebastian Argus-Report* and glanced idly through its pages. She was thinking that it was a gossipy little paper, compared to the newspapers she had grown up with, when the photograph of an elderly man caught her attention. "Bard to Appear" was the caption and beneath it, in smaller type, Shelley read, "Jonas Hornbostle, noted poet and winner of the Biddle Prize for Poetry, will appear at the Swancutt Hall of Music, Orange Belt College, Vincente, Saturday afternoon at two-thirty. Mr. Hornbostle will read from his own works, which include such distinguished works as *Litany for a Lizard* and *Prairie Depot*."

A real live poet, and Jonas Hornbostle at that! Shelley meditated on this bit of information. She had not realized that Jonas Hornbostle was still living—so many people whose works were required reading in English were dead. Jonas Hornbostle, whose poem, *Buffalo Bones*, was included in the textbook for English 5. Shelley preferred the poetry of Edna St. Vincent Millay, but she was impressed by

the works of Jonas Hornbostle, who rarely used rhyme
and who wrote so vigorously about earthy subjects.
Shelley examined his picture more closely. The poet
had a shock of unruly gray hair and heavy dark
eyebrows. The photograph revealed every pore and
every line in his face as he appeared to be squinting
into the sun at some distant object, an eagle perhaps.

Shelley dropped the paper. She knew exactly what
she was going to do. She was going to tell Hartley
that she intended to interview Jonas Hornbostle. If
she told him in the right way, perhaps he would suggest they go together to the Swancutt Hall of Music,
hear Jonas Hornbostle read his poetry, and then go
backstage to interview him. That would really be
something to write home about!

The next morning, in their registration room, Shelley turned around to Hartley the first thing and said,
"I have a marvelous idea for that interview assignment."

"Who's your victim?" asked Hartley.

"Jonas Hornbostle," Shelley announced.

"Hey!" exclaimed Hartley. "Smart girl! I read about
him in last night's paper and didn't even think about
interviewing him. I guess I thought he was too
famous."

"There is no reason why two members of the class
can't interview the same person, is there?" Shelley
hoped this would give Hartley the right idea.

"No, I guess not." Hartley frowned. "Darn it all,
anyway. This is the one Saturday afternoon that I
can't go. But it sure is a good idea and I wish you
luck. Meeting a famous poet should be interesting."

"Yes," agreed Shelley, with less enthusiasm. Somehow it had not occurred to her that she might have to
do this interview alone. She had counted on Hartley's
presence to give her courage, and now she was

frightened at the thought of facing the famous man without him.

"Be sure you let me read the interview before you hand it in," said Hartley. "I'd like to see it."

"Of course," agreed Shelley. Letting Hartley read her story should be an inspiration to her, because she would not want to show him a poor piece of work. She valued his opinion too much.

When Saturday afternoon arrived, Mavis's insistence that she take the station wagon rather than the bus added to Shelley's pleasure and excitement at the afternoon before her. It was one of those California days that seemed to belong to no season at all. She felt very mature to be driving alone past the groves where crews on ladders were picking oranges, past the used-car lots and the Giant Orange on her way to meet a famous poet. Mr. Hornbostle? My name is Shelley Latham, she would say. And he would answer, Shelley—a poet's name. Well, no, he probably wouldn't, because he was an earthy poet, but it would be nice if he did. And if he did, could she put it in the interview without sounding as if she were bragging? Yes, of course she could. Anything he said would be part of the interview. Such a remark was full of human interest and belonged in the interview with a real live poet. Accuracy, accuracy, accuracy Mrs. Boyce always stressed in journalism class. Shelley mentally sharpened a pencil and prepared to be accurate, accurate, accurate.

Shelley began to recite in ringing tones as she drove toward Vincente:

" 'Highway 30 bisects the sod where once they
    lay.
  Bison bones
  Bleached by sun, leached by rain. . . .' "

* * *

She wished she could remember more than the first
three lines of *Buffalo Bones*. What she did remember was looking up "leach" in the dictionary when
she studied the poem. It would be so much easier if
Jonas Hornbostle wrote poetry with a regular rhyme
scheme. Oh, well. " 'Highway 30 bisects the sod,' "
she repeated.

Driving to Vincente was easy enough, but finding
a parking space near the Orange Belt College was
not so easy. So many people had come into town to
shop on Saturday afternoon. Every time Shelley
thought she had found a place to park, the space
turned out to be occupied by a small foreign car.
Time was getting short and Shelley, eager for a good
seat, finally drove around behind the Swancutt Hall
of Music and held up honking traffic while someone
backed out of a space. Glad that the streets were wide
enough for diagonal parking, Shelley slid into the
space, jumped out of the station wagon and carefully
locked it before she ran around to the front of the
auditorium and up the steps to purchase her ticket
along with the rest of the crowd that had had difficulty finding parking space.

It was after two-thirty when Shelley slid past a
long line of knees and into a seat. The audience,
which was not as large as Shelley had expected for
such a famous man, appeared to be made up mostly
of college students and women who were removing
their flowery hats. Shelley had not seen so many hats
since she had come to California. As she sat down,
the president of the college was finishing his intro-
duction to the poet and the sound of applause gave
Shelley a moment to catch her breath.

Jonas Hornbostle rose from his chair, walked to
the lectern, laid down a sheaf of papers, removed a

spectacle case from his pocket, opened it, put on a pair of dark-rimmed spectacles, removed them, took a handkerchief from his pocket, and wiped each lens carefully, to a ripple of sympathetic laughter from the audience. Shelley settled back in her seat. She was, at last, in the presence of greatness. It was too bad Hartley could not be there to share the experience with her.

Jonas Hornbostle put on his spectacles, hesitated, removed them, and meticulously wiped the right lens to the accompaniment of more sympathetic laughter. At last the spectacles were settled on the bridge of his distinguished nose and Jones Hornbostle began to read. Shelley was thrilled. A truly famous man speaking famous lines and she was listening! And before the afternoon was over she, Shelley Latham, would actually speak to him. (Dear Rosemary, You'll never in a million years guess what I did today! I interviewed Jonas Hornbostle—you remember from English 5. Yes, little old me. I walked right up to him and . . .)

Shelley was only slightly disappointed when she had difficulty understanding Mr. Hornbostle. He did not exactly mumble, neither did he speak with an accent, but it was not easy to catch his words. The audience coughed a lot and that did not help. Even so, Shelley admired the poet wholeheartedly. That famous shock of gray hair, the loose knot in his tie, his suit rumpled as if greatness had no time for sending a suit out to be pressed. How wonderful it would be if he really did say, "Shelley? A poet's name." Shelley caught the familiar words, "Highway 30 bisects the sod," and a thrill went through her. Little had she dreamed when she was studying English 5 that someday . . .

Intermission came, and it occurred to Shelley that

from her present seat in the center of the auditorium she might have some difficulty reaching Mr. Hornbostle when his program was over. She peered around the auditorium for a seat on an aisle.

"Disgusting, isn't it?" Shelley was startled by a voice beside her. She had been only vaguely aware that the seat was filled. Now she turned to look at the fairly young man, probably a college student, who was sitting beside her.

"Disgusting?" she echoed. "What's disgusting?"

"Hornbostle. The whole performance," answered the young man who, like the poet, was wearing dark-rimmed glasses.

"Jonas Hornbostle?" asked Shelley, in the rising inflection of astonishment. Jonas Hornbostle disgusting? This man must be mad.

"Of course," answered the young man disagreeably. "Can you hear him?"

"Well, not every word, but—" admitted Shelley.

"You see?" said the young man. "The whole thing is an insult to your intelligence. He's really on exhibit."

Shelley looked shocked.

"Don't look that way," said the stranger impatiently. "What good is it to listen to a poet if you can't understand a word he says? And all that nonsense about wiping his glasses. I tell you he is just on exhibit. He and his manager think we are lucky people because we paid a dollar and a half plus tax just to look at him."

"But—" protested Shelley.

The young man was not going to listen to a protest. "Anyway," he went on, "just because he once wrote passable poetry doesn't necessarily mean he can read it."

Jonas Hornbostle's poetry *passable*? Shelley stared

at this person beside her, who by this time was collecting frowns as well as smiles of amusement from the other members of the audience.

"I'm glad I didn't waste my money on the LP record he made. I'll bet he's even worse on hi-fi," said the young man. Suddenly he rose from his seat. "I've had my intelligence insulted enough for one afternoon," he announced, and left.

At least Shelley was able to move one seat closer to the aisle. I don't care, she told herself. He *is* a famous man and his poetry *is* good and I *am* lucky to be listening to him and my intelligence feels just fine. But Shelley had difficulty even trying to listen to the second half of the reading. The moment of her interview was drawing closer. She folded back the cover of her notebook and fumbled in her purse to make sure she had not forgotten her pen. Mr. Hornbostle? I'm Shelley Latham. May I ask you a few questions for my school paper? She did not have to tell him that she was only a first-semester journalism student. First she would ask him a few factual questions to get him started talking and then she would ask what advice he had to give to students who wanted to write poetry. That would be the most important part of the interview. Accuracy, accuracy, accuracy, Shelley repeated to herself for reassurance and, from her journalism textbook, who, what, when, where, why?

Shelley sat on the edge of her seat waiting for the reading to end. She would have to move quickly to reach the poet before he left the auditorium. When at last applause filled the auditorium, Shelley did not wait for the clapping to subside before she whispered, "Excuse me, excuse me," and edged past knees and over toes to the aisle. She struggled against the tide of the departing audience and made her way to the front of the auditorium, where Mr. Hornbostle, a taller man than he had appeared to be from her seat, was surrounded by important-looking people who were, she supposed, members of the college faculty.

Shelley edged as close as she could. This was not going to be easy, she could see. Maybe she had better skip her name and start by asking questions. Still, she did not want to do that. She peered anxiously through the crowd at Mr. Hornbostle, who was busy signing autographs. He was considerably older than his photograph in the *Argus-Report* and he looked tired. The price of fame, thought Shelley.

When the last autograph was signed, and the last lady thanked for telling him she liked his poetry, and only a few members of the college faculty remained with the poet, Shelley clutched her courage, moistened her lips, stepped forward, and spoke to the man, who was about to leave. "Uh—Mr. Hornbostle?"

"Yes?" Was that impatience in his voice?

"My name is Shelley Latham." No response. "Could I—that is, do you have time to answer a few questions for my school paper?" Shelley sensed the amusement of the faculty members, but it was too late to back out now.

"Well?" said Jonas Hornbostle.

Apparently the poet meant this to be consent. At least he was looking at Shelley instead of moving toward the door. Encouraged, Shelley quickly decided she had no time for notes. She would have to remember what he said.

"Mr. Hornbostle, what do you think of Vincente—this part of the country?" she asked, looking up into the tired, impatient face.

"Does it matter what I think?" he asked ironically but not unkindly.

Shelley felt confused. Probably what he thought really did not matter, but that was not the sort of answer she expected him to give. "Well . . ." She gulped and tried frantically to think of a question that would sound intelligent and start him talking about himself. "Uh—how old were you when you wrote your first poem?"

Mr. Hornbostle raised one of his famous black eyebrows. "Poems?" he queried gently. "Have I written any? I am not so sure of that."

I'm getting no place fast, thought Shelley, uncomfortably aware that the college faculty members found the whole scene amusing. "Mr. Hornbostle," she began, determined that this time she was going to get a definite answer out of the man. "Where were you born?" That was a question that he could not evade.

Before Shelley's eyes the tired, impatient face grew more tired and more impatient. "My dear young reporter," said Jonas Hornbostle, "the answer to that question can be found in any one of a number of standard reference books that I am sure are available for your use in your school library. Have you never heard of *Who's Who in America?*"

"Yes," Shelley managed to whisper, unable to take her eyes from the poet's face. This could not be happening to her. No, no. Not to her. Things like this did not really happen. It *was* happening, though.

"Then if you expect to gain practice in interviewing, I would suggest that you never ask a question that can be answered in your library. *Who's Who in America* will not only tell you where I was born, it will also tell you how many children I have and give you their names. That, I presume, was to be your next question."

Shelley managed to tear her horrified gaze away from the famous face. She looked at the floor and whispered, "Thank you." Then, with tears in her eyes, she turned and walked halfway up the aisle until she could stand it no longer. She broke into a run and ran the rest of the way out of the building.

Safe inside the station wagon, Shelley sat trembling behind the steering wheel. Outside the world still seemed serene. A breeze moved the pendant branches of a pepper tree in front of the car, and down the block two little girls were playing hopscotch and laughing. Shelley rested her forehead on the steering wheel. What did I expect, she asked herself bitterly, the whole world to change because she had made a fool of herself in front of a famous man and a good part of the faculty of the Orange Belt College? And she had thought herself so smart, starting out to interview a celebrity. She had planned to impress Hartley and to knock the whole Journalism 1 class right back on its heels with her cleverness. And who got knocked back on her heels? Shelley Latham, the girl who was too stupid even to be a cub reporter. Shelley Latham, sub-cub, that was what she was. Whatever would she tell Hartley? She had promised to let him read her story and now there would be no story.

Shelley lifted her head from the steering wheel. She could not sit there all afternoon trying to pull herself together when Mavis was expecting her to return with the car. Automatically she inserted the key in the ignition and as she turned it, anger toward the poet swept over her. What a rude man he was! And where would he be without a public to admire him? And she had been his admirer. That was what hurt Shelley most—she had truly admired the poet, and then to have him be so curt to her . . .

Shelley drove slowly home and as she turned into the familiar streets of San Sebastian, the anger drained out of her and she felt suddenly very tired. She could no longer be angry with Jonas Hornbostle. He was right. It was she who had been rude in expecting a tired and busy man to take time to answer her inexpert questions. Why, in every town he visited he probably met at least one journalism student along with the autograph seekers and the ladies in flowery hats. And probably they all asked him the same questions.

The words of the young man who had sat beside her came back to Shelley and she now felt that perhaps he had been right after all. Jonas Hornbostle was a poor reader of his own poetry, and for that reason she began to feel sorry for him. It must be difficult to read badly in front of an audience and then to be pestered by journalism students. He had really not been angry with her so much as terribly, terribly weary.

Shelley turned into North Mirage Avenue and then into the Michies' driveway. She had failed. On Monday morning she would have to admit to Hartley that she had failed. Hartley, of all people. If he had gone to Vincente he would have come back with an interview. He would have gone prepared with a list of interesting and intelligent questions, because Hartley was the kind of boy who always knew exactly what he was doing.

Early Saturday evening the telephone rang. "It's for you, Shelley," said Katie. She added in a whisper, "It's a boy."

"Hello?" said Shelley, wondering what boy could be calling her. Maybe Philip's father had relented after all.

"Hi, Shelley," answered Hartley. "Did you get the interview?"

"No," answered Shelley reluctantly, but feeling that she might as well bring to an end the whole unpleasant incident as soon as possible. And just when she had succeeded in attracting Hartley's interest once more, too.

"How come?" There was disappointment in Hartley's voice. "Wouldn't he talk to you?"

"Oh, he talked to me all right," said Shelley, not wanting to admit what had happened.

"Well, come on, tell me about it," persisted Hartley. "If he talked to you, you must have an interview."

"Oh, no, I don't," said Shelley.

"What happened?" asked Hartley.

Shelley was silent a moment. "Wait a minute!" she exclaimed. "Maybe I do have a story after all." Briefly she described the episode. "And how do you think it would be," she concluded, "if I wrote it straight and told what really did happen? I mean, wouldn't that make a story?"

"Sure it would," said Hartley enthusiastically. "That would be a better story than if he had answered your questions straight."

"Do you really think so?" asked Shelley eagerly.

"I know it," said Hartley.

"Then I'll do it," said Shelley. "It will make me look like an awful idiot but I don't care."

"Don't worry about that," Hartley reassured her. "We all have to learn sometime and besides, the fact that you had a hard time asking questions will make a good angle. You know, a headline something like 'Famous Poet Gives Cub Reporter Lesson in Interviewing'."

"That's so," agreed Shelley. "I hadn't thought of that."

"Say, Shelley," said Hartley, as if he had just had another idea. "If you aren't doing anything this evening, maybe I could come over and help you write the story."

"Why—I'd love to have you come over," said Shelley truthfully. She had not expected this much.

"Swell. I'll be over in about an hour," said Hartley.

"Do you have a date?" asked Katie eagerly when Shelley had hung up. She had been following the conversation from the living room.

"Yes," said Shelley happily. "At least a sort of date. Hartley is coming over to help me with my journalism."

"That counts as a date," Katie assured her. "Would you like me to bake a cake?"

Shelley laughed. "I'm sure Hartley would enjoy a piece of cake."

"I can make cocoa, too," said Katie. "Like we made at school. Of course at school we called it breakfast cocoa but I don't see why it wouldn't taste all right at night."

"It will probably taste better," said Shelley. "And now I've got to change my dress." Blessings on thee, Jonas Hornbostle, thought Shelley, as she ran up the stairs to her room. Poor tired old poet.

Chapter 13

Dear Mother and Daddy, Shelley mentally wrote, as she opened the door for Hartley. This evening Hartley, the boy who took me to Vincente that time when I first came down here, came over to see me and we worked on our journalism assignment. . . .

"Hello, Shelley," said Hartley as he entered. "I hope you won't write like the *Argus-Report* and call a poet a bard."

Shelley laughed. " 'Bard' is a funny word to use, now that I stop to think about it, but the *Argus-Report* uses a lot of funny words. Like 'tot.' They use that a lot—I suppose because it is easy to fit into a headline."

"There is a 'Dog Bites Tot' or a 'Tot Lost' story in almost every issue," Hartley agreed with a grin.

Tom was attending a meeting and after greeting Hartley, Mavis excused herself, saying she was going to her studio. Shelley produced the rough draft of the interview that she had managed to write, and she and Hartley sat down in the living room at the long table below the handmade hooked rug that hung on the wall—Tom could not bear to see anyone walk on Mavis's hard work, so the Michies had hung the rug on the wall. Shelley felt perfectly natural sitting there with Hartley, almost as if they had sat there together often. This rather surprised her, but she decided she must feel at ease with him because he sat behind her in her registration room at school.

Shelley was not disturbed by Luke's sitting in his favorite chair studying a catalogue of motorcycle parts nor was she annoyed when Katie, in a fresh cotton dress, wandered in and out of the room. She was amused that Katie had dressed up for her date and she knew that Katie was interested in everything she and Hartley said. Katie was thinking that someday she could have a boy come over to study, too.

Hartley read Shelley's interview and they talked it over. He made suggestions, Shelley made suggestions, and they had one argument. Hartley thought that after the first sentence she should refer to Jonas Hornbostle as Mr. Hornbostle.

"But I never think of him as Mister," Shelley protested. "Of course I called him Mr. Hornbostle when I spoke to him, but writing is different. Nobody writes about a poet as Mister. They are called by their full names or just their last names."

"But he's a human being," Hartley pointed out. "Why shouldn't he be called Mister?"

"It doesn't sound right. Did you ever hear anyone call Shelley—Percy Bysshe, that is—Mr. Shelley?" Shelley asked. "Of course not. It is always just Shelley or Percy Bysshe Shelley."

"I guess that's right," admitted Hartley. "But on the other hand, I'm sure that I have read about T. S. Eliot as Mr. Eliot."

"That does sound sort of familiar." Shelley ran through the names of all the male poets she could think of. Browning, Keats, Longfellow, Sandburg—Mr. Sandburg? "Hartley, you're right!" she exclaimed, and wondered why she sounded triumphant when she had lost the argument. "It's dead poets that you don't call Mister. Jonas Hornbostle is alive so it is all right to call him Mister."

Together they rewrote the interview. Hartley read the new version. "That's good," he said seriously. "Mrs. Boyce should give you an A on it. It tells a lot about the poet—about his being tired and impatient and all, possibly because he knows he is not very good at reading his own poetry—most people don't think of a poet as being that human—and it tells what was wrong with a cub reporter's interview. It is different from most school interviews."

"Thank you, Hartley," said Shelley, pleased by his approval. "The *Bastion* does seem to publish a lot of silly interviews." She should know. She was still embarrassed by the memory of the interview she had given.

"A silly interview in the school paper is such a permanent fixture in San Sebastian that nobody really sees it any more," said Hartley jokingly, "just like—"

"—a cannon from the first World War in the park," finished Shelley.

"Exactly," agreed Hartley, laughing.

"When I first arrived I thought a cannon was such a funny thing to put in a park," Shelley said, "and now it seems a perfectly natural part of the landscape."

Luke closed his catalogue of motorcycle parts and stood up. "Good night," he said.

"Good night," said Shelley. "I hope we aren't driving you away."

"No," answered Luke good-naturedly. "I smelled cake baking and I thought I would see if Katie had taken it out of the oven yet."

The room was silent. Shelley and Hartley had no reason to discuss the interview any longer. Shelley looked at the boy beside her and a tiny thought, a thought that she felt was disloyal, intruded. It was a relief to be free of Ping-Pong, to sit and talk to a boy about something that interested them both, instead of batting that exasperating little ball back and forth. Why, I'm having fun, thought Shelley, surprised— more real fun than I ever had with Philip.

Katie appeared, bearing a tray with two pieces of cake and two cups of cocoa. Shelley, touched by the sight of her in her fresh dress and carefully cleaned shoes, said easily, "Katie, why don't you join us?" When Philip had come she had always wanted to show him off to Katie and then get him out of the way before Katie could do or say something awkward. It was different with Hartley. He would understand about Katie. Of course he would, and Shelley had been foolish not to explain about Katie on the refrigerator long ago.

Katie was obviously delighted to be invited to share Shelley's evening with a boy. She carried in another piece of cake and another cup of cocoa and sat down at the end of the long table.

"Blue frosting looks sort of funny on a cake," she said shyly. "I thought it would look prettier." She ate carefully, taking small bites and sitting up very straight. Just watching her made Shelley feel good.

"Blue frosting is good," said Hartley. "You could call it Surprise Frosting. Everyone expects something flavored with mint to be green so when you bite into blue frosting and find it mint-flavored, it is a surprise."

Shelley could see that Katie was pleased, and she knew that Hartley understood that Katie was thrilled to be included and was trying to act grown-up. Katie was even more pleased when Hartley ate a second piece of cake.

Shelley studied Hartley thoughtfully. She liked a

boy who would go out of his way to be nice to a junior-high-school girl. When they had finished eating they all carried their dishes into the kitchen. Hartley was the kind of boy who was at ease in the kitchen. He rinsed and stacked the plates as if working at the Michies' sink was the most natural thing in the world. It was easy to picture him helping with a batch of fudge and enjoying himself if a girl could think of no better way to entertain a boy.

When they had finished with the dishes, Shelley and Hartley returned to the living room. Katie went upstairs to her room, and from the garage came intermittent pop-pops from Luke's motorcycle. At last Shelley felt that she could talk freely to Hartley. "Do you remember that night we went to Vincente to eat the doughnut holes?" she asked, determined to be forthright.

"Of course. The night you talked about the pomegranates," said Hartley. "Does San Sebastian still seem like a beautiful place to you after the smudging we went through?"

Shelley spoke seriously. "It was unpleasant at the time, but you know, I think it was exciting the way the whole town cared about the oranges. Every time I eat an orange I'll think about that cold spell and the way the boys who worked in the groves came to school greasy and tired and fell asleep in class and the teachers didn't even say anything. I've never lived where people were concerned about crops before. I mean, I have read about damage to wheat or something in the papers, but I never understood how the people felt before."

Shelley was silent for a moment. She wanted to bring the conversation to its starting point. She looked straight into Hartley's dark eyes. "I've always wanted to explain why I acted so sort of funny when we said good night that time after we went to Vincente," she said, and noticed Hartley suddenly look as if he were on his guard. She did not care. She had to explain, because the matter had been on her conscience so long. "That night I happened to look up and see Katie looking through the open transom—you know how the refrigerator is against the door we never use between the living room and the kitchen. She was kneeling on top of the refrigerator watching us say good night so she would learn how to act when she has dates. I was so embarrassed I—well, I just acted funny, is all. It seems silly now, but that is the way it was."

Hartley threw back his head and laughed. "So that's what was the matter! I didn't know why you were suddenly acting so stiff and formal. I thought you had had a good time and I didn't know what was wrong. I thought maybe you didn't like it when I came right out and said I liked you so soon, or something."

"Oh, no," said Shelley, relieved that she had finally explained. "I was terribly pleased to come to a strange town and get to know a boy who liked me right off."

"And then you seemed so interested in Phil," Hartley went on, "that I didn't feel I should ask you for another date."

"I was interested in him," admitted Shelley, looking down at the table. This was touching on a painful subject. "He is one of the nicest fellows I have ever known, but I don't know—I guess we don't have an awful lot in common." Until Shelley spoke the words it had never occurred to her that she and Philip did not have much in common. They had really found very little to talk about. She had not enjoyed Philip himself as much as the admiration of the other girls who liked him and the thought that he looked like the kind of boy her mother would like her to know.

She frowned a moment before she said, "You know, now I'm not sure it was Philip I liked so much after all. I think maybe it was just that I saw him that first day of school and I was so excited to be in San Sebastian with real palm trees and oranges growing on trees and everything. He was so good-looking I just thought he was the boy I had always wanted to meet. In my mind I turned him into the boy I wanted him to be. And he wasn't at all. He doesn't even want to go to college. I really feel sorry for him." She stopped, afraid she might have said too much. She did not want to criticize Philip.

Hartley raised one eyebrow and said wickedly, "You looked at me the first day of school, too."

"I don't mean that you aren't good-looking, too," Shelley said hastily. "You are, you know, in a different way."

Hartley grinned at Shelley, enjoying her discomfort. "I understand exactly what you mean about Philip. And you know something else? I think maybe you liked him because he was not the boy at home you were telling me about—the one who always said, 'Penny for your thoughts.' "

"I guess you're right," said Shelley thoughtfully.

Hartley leaned closer and spoke softly. "I still like you, Shelley."

Shelley looked into Hartley's serious brown eyes and was ashamed. She had maneuvered this evening just so she could write to her mother about another boy to make her mother think she had lost interest in Philip because of Hartley. She was trying to use him to shield her own mistake. And that was all wrong.

"I like you, too, Hartley," said Shelley honestly, realizing how much she really did like him. How foolish she had been not to understand this before.

Little things should have told her, things like her boredom with Ping-Pong and the way she rushed to confide in Hartley about her D in biology because she knew he would understand how important good grades were. She recalled a remark Mavis had made about the boy she called the Great White Hunter, something about girls in their teens always fancying themselves in love with the wrong boy. Shelley had not really fancied herself in love with Philip—her feeling had been excitement at knowing a new boy and pride in showing others that he liked her—but now she understood what Mavis meant.

Hartley put his hand over Shelley's. "Good," he said. "We like each other. That make it unanimous."

Shelley laughed. "Two votes and it is unanimous." She felt a sudden urge to talk to Hartley about everything in the world—school, and their plans for the future, and people they had known, and the mistakes they had made that had once seemed painful and now seemed funny. She wanted to make up for all the time they had lost.

But as Shelley sat with Hartley's hand over hers, she was disturbed by an elusive unhappy feeling. She liked Hartley, but Philip still liked her. Poor Philip, who had flunked biology and lost his chance to play basketball because of her.

Chapter 14

Spring, warm and gaudy, came to San Sebastian. One day was no season at all and the next day was spring —a spring unlike any Shelley had ever known. Wild flowers bright as paint spilled by children colored the hills. Geraniums washed clean of dust bloomed brilliantly while vines and low plants that clung to the ground brought forth crimson and magenta flowers that shimmered in the bright spring light. The orange trees, covered with bridal blossoms, filled the town with rich perfume. Shelley had not known that anything in the world could be as fragrant as San Sebastian in the spring.

The perfume of the groves grew stronger at night and as she lay in bed consciously enjoying every breath, Shelley thought how different this was from spring at home. An Oregon spring meant fresh green leaves unfolding on the birch trees that lined Shelley's street. It meant rain soft as pussy willows and fat robins pulling worms out of the wet lawn. It meant trilliums in the woods and lilies of the valley in the back yard. Shelley was happy, now that she was rid of homesickness, to lie in bed and enjoy two springs, gaudy and delicate, one in reality and the other in memory.

Hartley replaced Philip on Saturday nights and Shelley was not sorry. She felt gloriously free of that plonking little Ping-Pong ball. When she and Hartley discovered they both enjoyed working double-crostics, they spent several evenings prowling through the Michies' reference books trying to find Cotton Mather's wife's maiden name or a colloquial expression of three words meaning to be in good health—the second letter had to be *n* and the last letter *k*. Shelley was delighted. She had always enjoyed puzzles and word games but she had not expected a boy to enjoy them too.

Once when one of the puzzles called for the name of the chief room in a Roman house, Shelley printed the word *atrium* in the proper spaces and was reminded of her first school dance a long time ago. "Hartley, is this a peculiar way to spend an evening?" she asked suddenly.

"Of course not," he answered. "We're both having fun. Why do you even ask?"

"I was just thinking about the first time I ever went to a school dance," she explained. "I went with a boy from my Latin class, the studious type, and we spoke Latin as much as we could."

Hartley laughed delightedly. "Whatever did you find to say?"

Shelley giggled. "I don't suppose our conversation was exactly witty. I remember saying that the floor of the gymnasium was divided into three parts. You know, like all Gaul in Caesar, but I had to cheat a little, because I didn't know the Latin for 'gymnasium,' so I just pronounced it with what I hoped was a Latin accent. And we said things like, '*Is* drummer *cum diligentia laborat.*'"

"Don't all drummers work diligently?" Hartley asked, laughing.

Shelley laughed with him. "It was funny, wasn't it?" she remarked, thinking that now the whole incident seemed like something that had happened a long time ago when she was practically a child, and she wondered why she had been so upset by her mother's amusement. Because she had felt so unsure of herself, probably.

Shelley enjoyed Hartley's companionship. Once he arrived late in the morning with a picnic lunch and drove Shelley to the mountains to see the wild lilac covered with blossoms the color of blue smoke. They picnicked beside a stream. "So you can see that we really do have water in California," Hartley explained. Shelley, who had always had to pack the lunch when she picnicked with a boy, was charmed. She did not, however, talk about her dates with Hartley to any of the girls at school except Jeannie. She could not help feeling guilty, with Philip working doggedly beside her in the biology laboratory and—she supposed— studying with equal doggedness at home on week ends. When Hartley asked her to go to the school carnival with him, Shelley accepted although she did not feel quite right about it, knowing that Philip could not go.

It was on the Saturday of the carnival that Shelley received a letter from her mother in the same mail in which Mavis received a letter from her mother, Mrs. Stickney.

Shelley's letter concluded with a worrisome paragraph. "Jack came over this evening," Mrs. Latham wrote. "I was so glad to see him. He is such a nice boy and I have missed him while you have been away. He wanted to know when you would be home. I told him Daddy and I were going to drive down to get you and that we planned to take in Yosemite and the redwoods on the way home but we expected to be back the end of June. He was pleased to hear this and said he wanted you to go to the mountains with him and his family over the Fourth of July."

Jack. Shelley read the paragraph again. Her mother did not say she had accepted the invitation for Shelley, but Shelley was sure she had. Naturally her mother would not want to see her sitting at home on a day when other girls would be away on picnics or trips to the beach or mountains. But Jack—oh, well, as Rosemary said, a boy in the hand was worth two in the bush or any old port in a storm. But Shelley was not entirely successful in persuading herself that this was true. She might have believed it at one time but not since knowing Hartley. However, if her mother had accepted for her, there was not much she could do about it but go to the mountains with Jack and his family. She knew what it would be like, though. A crowd of people would come up from the city and there would be whispered questions about Shelley and Jack. Jack's mother would smile and whisper that Shelley and Jack were going steady. Everyone would smile back and there would be half-heard remarks about that was the way kids did things these days— now when I was in high school . . . Shelley would hate every minute of it.

"Goodness!" exclaimed Mavis, looking up from her letter. "Mother will arrive this week end. Honestly, I can't understand why she absolutely refuses to send letters airmail." There was considerable exasperation in her voice. "Shelley, I wonder if you would mind picking some fresh flowers for the dining room and for the coffee table while I make up the bed in the corner bedroom. Mother is apt to turn up at any hour of the day or night."

"I'll be glad to," said Shelley, and went about the pleasant task. She chose some wild California poppies that were blooming among the weeds at the back of the Michies' property and arranged some of them in a brown mug that Mavis had made. The rest she set in a green pitcher of Mexican glass for the dining-room table. She was pleased with the effect of both her arrangements. They were gay and casual, suited to the Michie household.

Not long after Shelley had finished with the flowers, an old car pulled into the driveway with a crunch of tires on gravel.

"Hello, Mother!" called Mavis from an upstairs window. "I'll be right down."

Shelley joined the family at the side of the house, where a tall gray-haired woman was getting out of the car. It was obvious that she knitted. While Mrs. Stickney kissed her daughter and grandchildren, Shelley stared at her dress. It was knit round and round in random stripes of yarn of every imaginable color.

"That's some dress you are wearing," remarked Tom, after he had hugged his mother-in-law.

"I call it my coat of many colors," replied Mrs. Stickney. "I told myself there must be something I could knit out of all those odds and ends of yarn, so I knit this. It's the most practical thing in the world for traveling. Nothing shows on it and I just keep turning the skirt around and it never bags in the seat."

"That's my girl," said Tom, and kissed Mrs. Stickney on her cheek. "Luke, get your grandmother's luggage out of the car."

"And this is Shelley," said Mrs. Stickney, taking Shelley's hand in hers.

"How do you do?" said Shelley, as she took her eyes off the fascinating dress.

While Luke pulled three suitcases out of the car, and a large knitting bag that Katie eyed with distrust, Mavis said, "Mother, aren't you ever going to get a new car? That one is so old I worry about your driving it on the highway."

"Nonsense," said Mrs. Stickney. "I understand that car and that car understands me."

"It's a car, Mother," said Mavis. "Not a horse."

"Anyway," said Mrs. Stickney, "if I keep it long enough, some old car collector is bound to offer me a lot of money for it." It was easy to see she was a woman with a mind of her own.

The afternoon seemed unusually lively, even for the Michies, so lively that Shelley had little time to think about her mother's letter. First of all Shelley was dismayed to see that the poppies she had arranged so carefully had folded their petals as if it were night and instead of two gay bouquets, they became stiff bunches of pointed buds. Probably in protest against being picked, Shelley decided.

"That's all right," said Mavis. "Just put them in a dark cupboard for a while and they will open up when you bring them out into the light."

Amused at the idea of trying to outwit flowers, Shelley did as she was told. This crazy mixed-up California vegetation!

After Mrs. Stickney had unpacked, she settled herself with her knitting needles and some bright green yarn which Katie could not help staring at so apprehensively that Shelley, to end her suspense, finally came right out and asked Mrs. Stickney what she was knitting.

"A pull-over for Luke," she answered. "I am making it out of his school colors."

Shelley and Katie exchanged a look of conspiracy, while Luke's expression became worried. Only letter men wore sweaters in school colors but a grandmother could not be expected to know that.

"Luke, what are you up to these days?" asked Mrs. Stickney, pausing to measure her knitting.

"I'm helping Dad in the grove and using the money I earn for parts for my motorcycle," answered Luke. "I'll get it running one of these days."

"Now, Luke," protested Mavis. "We've been through this a dozen times. You're just wasting money on that old wreck and even if you do get it to run, which I doubt, you are too young to get a license."

"Nonsense," said Mrs. Stickney. "The boy has to grow up."

"I'm going to be sixteen," Luke told his mother.

Mavis looked as if she were about to say something but thought better of it. Instead she told Katie that she had to practice her piano lesson, both the rhapsody and her scales, before she could go over to Pamela's house. Katie observed that she never had any fun and began to play the *Hungarian Rhapsody*. Suddenly, as if she had had an inspiration, she speeded up her playing until the music sounded as if it were being rattled out by an old-fashioned player piano.

"Katie!" shouted Tom in his basketball-court voice.

The playing stopped. "Mommy said I had to play it through before I could go over to Pamela's," answered Katie plaintively.

"Now Katie," said Tom. "Time is just as much a part of the music as the notes. You know that. Now play it properly."

The music continued with only one lapse into *Pop Goes the Weasel*. Then Katie went to work on her scales. Shelley was the only one who noticed an open copy of *Betsy Devore, Girl Sleuth* resting on the music rack while Katie's fingers flew up and down the keyboard.

When Mavis went into the kitchen to put the roast into the oven, Mrs. Stickney went along to visit with her daughter. Soon Shelley heard their voices rising through the transom.

"Mother, I know what I am doing," said Mavis. "This isn't the first roast I have ever cooked, you know."

"Mavis, I have been cooking roasts longer than you have," said Mrs. Stickney, "and I can't bear to see you ruin that meat."

"I know you have been cooking longer than I," said Mavis. "And sometimes the roasts were too rare and sometimes they were overdone. That is why I am doing it scientifically. By inserting a meat thermometer into the roast I can tell exactly when the meat is medium-rare."

"If you plunge that dagger into the bosom of that roast," said Mrs. Stickney dramatically, "all the juice will run out."

"Oh, Mother," said Mavis, and laughed.

Things were equally lively at dinner. The roast was excellent. The confused poppies opened their petals when brought from the cupboard as if they were greeting the morning sun. Everyone argued with everyone else.

Katie said it was Luke's turn to feed the dog and cat, because she fed them the night before. Luke said it was Katie's turn, because the only reason she fed them the night before was that the night before *that* he fed them when it was really her turn and she had gone off to that creep Pamela's house and he couldn't let the animals starve, could he? Shelley said she would be glad to feed the animals if it would settle the argument. Luke and Katie told her to please keep out of their affairs. Mrs. Stickney said when she was a girl, children did their chores cheerfully and did not argue at the table. Mavis said she and her brother always argued at the table and every place else. They still did. Tom told Katie to feed the cat and Luke to feed the dog and now couldn't they introduce a new topic of conversation?

They did. Mrs. Stickney said she was thinking of a trip to France next year—she had always wanted to see the château country. Mavis asked her mother please to promise not to ride a bicycle in France, not at her age. Mrs. Stickney said nonsense, she might be getting on in years but her bones were not that brittle yet.

Tom changed the subject by asking his mother-in-law who she thought would be elected the next president. Mrs. Stickney said she did not believe in discussing politics, especially with relatives, but . . . Mavis did not agree. She believed the man was more important than the party, but . . . Katie said her social-science teacher, who was not even supposed to discuss politics in the public schools, said . . . Luke said Katie was only in junior high and what did she know about it anyway? His history teacher said if a man was to be elected president it was essential that he be born east of the Rocky Mountains. Mrs. Stickney said that was nonsense. The way the West was expanding, it was high time the East realized the United States included the West.

"Whew!" exclaimed Shelley, when supper was over and she and Hartley were on their way to the carnival which was being held on the school's tennis courts. "I didn't know families could argue so much. And the funny part of it is, the Michies argue a lot but it never really seems to make any difference."

"I guess that's the way it is with families. Some families, anyway," said Hartley. "My dad and my brothers and I are always hacking away at one another but it doesn't really mean anything except maybe that we like one another. It would be different if we all kept still."

"I suppose," said Shelley thoughtfully, "that when there are a lot of arguments going on, no single one seems so important." She rode in silence awhile before she said, "I got into the silliest argument with my mother once over a raincoat. At least it seems silly now. I got so mad I stuffed a whole bouquet of fresh roses into the Disposall and ground them up."

"Why, Shelley," said Hartley, after they had laughed together over the incident, "you always seem so composed, it is hard to picture you doing such a thing."

"I guess I usually seethe within, but that time I boiled over," said Shelley, as Hartley parked the car near the tennis courts. She could laugh about the incident now, but could she, she wondered, when she returned home? She hoped so but she was not sure.

The tennis courts were a square of light in the fragrant night. Music poured forth from loud-speakers and mingled with the shouts and laughter of the crowd that wandered from one booth to another eating candied apples and popcorn, yelling encouragement or derision at those who were trying their skills at various booths.

When Shelley and Hartley entered the tennis courts, Shelley wondered a little uneasily what others would think at seeing her with Hartley when Philip had to stay home. Then she told herself she was worrying unnecessarily. Philip had never said anything about going steady, had he? But she could not help feeling that she would have a better time if Philip were here, with his usual crowd of boys—or even with another girl.

Shelley and Hartley wandered about, pausing to watch the boys from the print shop fill orders for calling cards, lingering at the nail-driving booth. "Oh, look," cried Shelley as they moved on. "The Gavel Club is selling personalized shrunken heads—it says so on that sign."

"The debaters must have been hard up for something to sell," remarked Hartley, as they walked across the tennis courts to look at the shrunken heads.

"Step right up, folks!" yelled the barker. "Have you ever wanted to shrink the head of one of your teachers? Don't miss this golden opportunity, the chance of a lifetime! Just twenty-five cents, one quarter of a dollar! Get your shrunken heads here!"

The heads were walnuts with faces painted on the wrinkled brown shells and black string glued to the top for hair. Hartley bought one of the heads, wrote something on the attached tag, and presented it to Shelley.

Shelley laughed when she saw Mr. Ericson's name on the tag. "Since I got ninety-six on that last quiz, I'm not anxious to shrink his head," she said, "but I'll take this home as a souvenir of San Sebastian."

Shelley and Hartley wandered on to the Block S Club's booth, one of the most popular concessions at the carnival. Members of the football team were taking turns wearing a helmet and poking their heads through a hole in a blanket. Students bought three balls for a dime and tried to hit the football player's helmet before he could duck. Shouts went up when a ball slammed against the top of a helmet. The crowd booed when the player ducked out of the way of the ball. Hartley paid his dime and picked up three balls. The first hit the blanket to the left of the player. The second was close but landed to the right. The crowd booed, and Hartley took careful aim. The third ball landed square on top of the helmet. Shelley cheered with the rest of the crowd. One of the nicest things about Hartley was that he did everything well, even throwing a ball at a carnival.

"Hartley, do you suppose I could hit a football player?" Shelley asked.

Hartley laughed. "I don't know, but you could try." He laid down a dime for Shelley's three balls.

"I'll bet she can't even hit the blanket," said one of the girls in the crowd.

Shelley laughed, picked up a ball, and threw as hard as she could. It hit the blanket, but that was about all you could say for it. The football player laughed at her. The crowd groaned. "She throws like a girl," someone commented.

"Well—I *am* a girl," said Shelley, and picked up her second ball. This time the football player grinned at her and did not even bother to duck. "Hey," protested Shelley. "Don't just stand there sneering. It's bad for my morale."

She aimed carefully the third time and came close enough so that the football player was able, by straining against the blanket, to lean over to the right and bump his head against the ball.

"See?" crowed Shelley. "I hit him."

"With a lot of co-operation from your target," scoffed someone.

"Shelley is an excellent shot," said Hartley. "She just has an individual style."

"Thanks, Hartley," said Shelley, flushed and laughing. Then as they started to leave, because the crowd was growing, they turned and found themselves face to face with Jeannie and Philip. Shelley stopped in surprise when she saw Philip, but the surprise did not last. Of course Philip had to go out sometimes. A boy's father could not keep him prisoner because he flunked biology. She should have known that.

Philip's face turned red with embarrassment. Shelley was aware that the crowd was watching to see what her reaction would be. Jeannie was looking at her and at Philip with bright-eyed interest, a little detached as if she were observing a scene instead of taking part in it. Shelley found that her only reaction was one of relief. Philip was not shut up at home with a pile of books while she was out having a good time. "Hi," she said, feeling uncomfortable only because so many people were watching. "Having fun?"

"Uh—Shelley," Philip began. "Jeannie and I got together at the library so she could go over my biology notebook before Mr. Ericson looks at it and then we—we decided to drop in here for a few minutes." Those were the words Philip spoke. He was silently asking Shelley not to mind.

"I'm glad you came," Shelley answered sincerely. "We've been having a lot of fun." She was happy to see the tense look on Philip's face relax. Now she knew where they stood. It was over for both of them. She need no longer have that vague, guilty feeling that had bothered her so often when she was with Hartley. Shelley's heart was light as she turned to Jeannie and said, "I hope you have as much fun as we've had."

Jeannie smiled and her eyes told Shelley how happy she was to be with Philip. It was a look that only another girl could appreciate. Philip looked at Shelley and gave her his slow, shy grin, a grin that no longer made Shelley catch her breath. It was just a nice smile from a boy whom she had once liked and still liked, but in a different way.

"I just hit a football player," said Shelley.

"Jeannie, do you want to try?" asked Philip.

"Good luck!" said Shelley.

Hartley put his hand on Shelley's elbow to guide her through the crowd. "You really didn't mind what happened, did you?" he remarked into her ear, when they had left Jeannie and Philip.

Shelley smiled over her shoulder at him. "I'm glad," she said honestly, and when they were out of the crowd she faced Hartley and said, "I guess I have felt sort of guilty about Philip. As if it were my fault he flunked biology and was not allowed to date or play on the basketball team. And now I don't feel that way any more." Shelley knew that she had been mistaken to have felt that way in the first place. Philip had earned his F the same way she had earned her D —he had not studied enough. His grades were not her responsibility.

Perhaps the whole unhappy incident was really for the best. If it had not happened she would have gone on dating Philip and eventually, because he was not really the boy she had wanted him to be, she would have come to feel about him the way she felt about Jack. Not that Philip would have said, "Penny for your thoughts." It would have been something else that he did—ordering those greasy grilled peanut-butter sandwiches, probably—that she would wish he would not do, and then she would know that she was tired of him. And by that time it would have been too late. Everyone would have assumed they were going steady, and her beautiful year in San Sebastian would have ended in disappointment.

"I know what," said Hartley. "Let's get out of this madhouse and drive over to Vincente for some doughnut holes."

"In memory of our first date," agreed Shelley. It was all over with Philip now and she knew that her year would not end on an unhappy note. Her wonderful year that made her feel as if she were seeing the world for the first time. Because she was so happy, she smiled at Hartley, suddenly and radiantly.

He looked down at her with a mixture of tenderness and amusement. "You always have fun, don't you, Shelley?" he asked.

"Yes," Shelley answered, as the noise and the crowd of the carnival became a bright spot behind them in the darkness, and the perfume of the orange blossoms hung heavy on the night. "Yes, I do have fun." And that was the way it should be when a girl was sixteen.

It was then that Shelley knew that she was not going to the mountains with Jack and his family over the Fourth of July, no matter what her mother had said. She would write him a nice note. . . .

She did not have time to think about the note, though. Hartley leaned over and kissed her on the tip of her nose.

Chapter 15

Suddenly the days were going much too fast for Shelley. She wanted to catch each hour and hold it just a little longer. The green hills were turning to gold, the sky was blue, laced with the vapor trails of jet planes, and Shelley's spirits were high.

Shelley found that even biology, after weeks of memorizing definitions and classifications, became interesting. When the class reached the chapter on heredity, she was fascinated. It seemed marvelous to her that Luther Burbank could decided that he wanted a large white daisy with a smooth stem and by working with three different flowers from three different continents, could in fifteen years of controlled breeding, produce the Shasta daisy, which was exactly what he wanted. If Luther Burbank had wanted a California poppy that would stay open after being picked, he could have bred one by crossing the sleepy poppy with some wide-awake variety.

Journalism was Shelley's favorite subject and when the Journalism 1 class put out the cub issue of the *Bastion*, Hartley was chosen editor—an honor that certainly meant he would be made editor of the paper in his senior year. Shelley had been made feature editor because Mrs. Boyce had been so pleased with her interview with Jonas Hornbostle. It was fun to stay after school working on the paper in the untidy room that students had decorated with signs that said, "Thimk" or "Don't just do something—stand there." It was fun because she and Hartley were sharing a real interest. Each moment spent bending over the dummy of the cub issue was precious.

The one flaw in Shelley's happiness was the thought of leaving San Sebastian so soon. She tried to stuff this thought into the back of her mind and slam a door on it, but the thought slipped out at the most inconvenient times. When Hartley tossed a paper from another high school onto her desk and asked her what she thought of its feature page, she picked it up and looked at it but she had trouble really seeing it. She was thinking that this was probably the last time in her whole life that Hartley would toss a paper onto her desk. Surely something would happen to spare her having to say good-by to him. If only she had not wasted so many months before getting to know him better!

The same sort of thought pursued Shelley at the Michies', too. When a letter arrived from home, Shelley's first thought was, Only two or three more letters from home before I have to say good-by to Hartley. When she joined Tom and his two children in packing their lunches for the next day, she thought, only ten more lunches on the lawn with Jeannie before I have to say good-by to Hartley. When Luke and Katie argued over whose turn it was to feed the animals, Shelley counted the number of times that were left for her to hear this argument.

When Katie began to talk about the last dancing class of the season, the class that was to be a party, Shelley shared her anticipation, hoping that this time Katie would not return from the party dejected because there were not enough boys to go around, or because all the boys were too short, or because Pamela had danced three times with Rudy while she had to dance with a boy with clammy hands, whose shoes made black marks all over her new white slippers.

It was over Katie's last dancing class that a crisis arose in the Michie household. Two days before the party Katie discovered that she had outgrown her best dress. Naturally she had to have a new dress. Katie requested what she called a store-boughten dress. Mavis said she could make a dress for half the price of a ready-made garment, and wouldn't Katie like yellow organdy? Katie said she would die, absolutely *die*, before she would go to the party in any old organdy dress. Organdy was for kindergarten. Mrs. Stickney suggested white dotted swiss. Dotted swiss was always so sweet, she thought. Katie did not actually disagree with her grandmother. She merely stared at the corner of the living-room ceiling with a stubborn, sulky look on her face.

A last dancing class was so important, and Shelley wanted so much for Katie to have a good time. "Maybe white piqué would be nice," she suggested cautiously.

"Yes!" agreed Katie enthusiastically, to everyone's relief. There was some argument over the pattern, but they finally settled on a princess style because there was no sash across the back. Katie would absolutely die before she would wear a dress with a sash to the party. She did not want any old ruffle around the neck, either.

Saturday morning passed in a flurry of pattern and material on the dining-room table and basting threads on the living-room rug, while both Mavis and Mrs. Stickney worked on the dress. When they were both busy sewing, Katie called Shelley into the laundry. "Shelley," she whispered, "can't you persuade Mommy to let me get a permanent? There is still time before the party and maybe she would listen to you."

Shelley was in a difficult position. She felt that straight hair was more becoming to Katie, whose face was round, and she knew Mavis would agree. At the same time she wanted Katie to feel she looked her best that evening.

"Please, Shelley," pleaded Katie.

"Katie, you know it wouldn't do any good," said Shelley, and then she had an inspiration. "Why don't you ask your mother if you could have your hair cut in a beauty shop?"

Katie was elated with this suggestion. Her mother and grandmother agreed that a professional haircut was a good idea, and for once something was accomplished without argument. Shelley made an appointment for Katie and drove her downtown in the station wagon because Mavis and Mrs. Stickney were too busy sewing. Katie emerged from the beauty shop with her hair thinned and trimmed into a sleek little cap.

"Katie, you look darling!" exclaimed Shelley. She could tell that Katie was pleased by the way she held her head higher as if she were proud of it.

Somehow Katie's dress was ready to try on and Mavis was marking the hem with a yardstick and a row of pins ("Katie, stand still. How do you expect me to get this hem straight when you stand first on one foot and then the other?") when from the garage came a loud popping noise and then the unmistakable sound of a motorcycle running.

"Luke's motorcycle!" cried Katie. "He's finally got it to run!" She jumped down from the stool she was standing on and ran to the window.

"There he goes down the driveway!" Shelley was excited over Luke's success after all these months.

"Oh!" The exclamation escaped Mavis as if this were the last straw.

The motorcycle turned at the corner of the house,

crossed the front lawn, proceeded under the pergola, and around to the back yard and the garage once more. The whole family was on the back porch when Luke arrived, grimy and triumphant, his face and hands smudged with grease. He stopped, with the motor idling. "She runs!" he shouted.

"Oh, I never thought ——" began Mavis.

"Well done, son," said Tom. "I never thought you'd do it but I'm proud of you."

"But he can't ride it," insisted Mavis. "He isn't old enough to have a license."

"I can ride it on our own property if I don't take it out on the road," Luke informed his mother, with the air of a boy who had inquired into the subject. "And next month I will be sixteen and can get a license."

"But Luke," protested Mavis, "I can't bear to think of you riding that dangerous contraption on the highway."

Luke looked stubborn.

"If the State of California lets him have a license to operate the motorcycle and Luke can earn enough money to support it, we will have to let him ride it," said Tom. "What is there for a boy his age to do? I would rather have him tinkering on a motorcycle than hanging around the drugstore like some boys."

"That's right, Mavis," agreed Mrs. Stickney. "You have to let your children grow up, you know."

"Sure, Mommy," said Katie. "He'll be all right."

"Sure I will," said Luke.

"But he's——" Mavis began. She stopped, defeated.

"We can only hope that we have brought him up to have enough sense to use his head," said Tom.

"I hope we have." Mavis managed a shaky smile.

"Mommy, my *hem*!" cried Katie. "We've got to finish my hem."

"This seems to be one of those days. If it isn't one thing it is another," said Mavis with a sigh. "Come on. I'll have to start pinning it all over after the way you have been jumping around."

Somehow, while Luke rode his motorcycle around and around the house, Katie's dress was finished and a meal prepared. After supper Katie showered, admired her hair frequently in the mirror, slipped her dress on over her best petticoat, and was ready for the party. She twirled around in front of her family. "Mommy, I just *love* my dress," she exclaimed. "And you know what? Pamela's mother can't sew a *thing*. She's awfully dumb about a lot of things."

"I am glad you are pleased, Katie," said Mavis. "But I don't think you should talk about Pamela's mother that way." Mavis sat down, rested her head on the back of the chair, and closed her eyes. "Shelley, is Hartley coming over this evening?" she asked.

"Not till later," answered Shelley. "Probably not till nine o'clock. They are having a family dinner for his grandmother's birthday and he has to stay around."

"Would you mind driving Katie to the party?" Mavis asked. "I'm too tired."

"I would love to," answered Shelley, who enjoyed driving.

When she had deposited Katie at the junior-high-school auditorium, Shelley said, "Have fun!"

"I will," said Katie, smiling. Then she turned and ran toward the auditorium before she remembered how grown-up she was and slowed down to a walk.

Shelley drove slowly back to the Michies', looking at all that had grown familiar in the last months—the cannon in the park, the big old houses along the main street, the high school's mission tower that had never contained a bell, the pomegranate trees, the groves that had shed their petals. She must remember every bit of it always.

At the Michies' Tom and Luke were washing the dishes while Mavis and her mother recovered from their frantic day of sewing. Mrs. Stickney's bright green yarn lay in her lap and everyone seemed too tired to argue about anything.

Shelley decided to go to her room to answer her mother's letter. She picked it up and glanced through it once more. "We are looking forward so much to our trip to California. We can hardly wait to see our daughter again. It seems as if you have been gone more than nine months. Mavis writes that Hartley is one of the nicest boys she has ever known and that is such a relief. I do worry so about you way off down there. What has happened to Philip?"

Shelley's feelings were a mixture of tenderness and irritation. Honestly, the way her mother acted as if she were still a child! Shelley picked up her pen and stared thoughtfully at a blank piece of notebook paper. "Dear Mother and Daddy," she began. "Of course Hartley is a nice boy. I don't know why you think I would be interested in any other kind. You really did not need to write for references—"

Shelley sat with her pen poised above the paper. She did not want to bicker with her mother, any more than her mother wanted to bicker with her. She could not understand why they behaved the way they did. She wished the situation would be different when she returned but she was afraid it would not. Her mother would still tell her she should wear the blue dress instead of the green or the green instead of the pink, she would still insist on helping Shelley select her clothes, she would still say she thought Shelley should not go over to Rosemary's house so often. And Shelley would still object to everything her mother said. She laid down her pen. Darn it all, anyway. Why did things have to be the way they were?

A little before eight-thirty Shelley went downstairs and asked, "Would you like me to go get Katie?"

"Why don't we all three go?" suggested Mavis. "Mother, wouldn't you enjoy a little ride?"

"I think it is a fine idea after such a hard day," agreed Mrs. Stickney.

"Oh, I forgot," said Mavis, when they arrived at the junior-high school and saw no sign that the party was ending. "Since this is the last class of the season, it lasts until nine o'clock." They sat in silence in the station wagon awhile until Mavis said, "Let's go in and watch. The girls always look so pretty in their spring dresses."

Shelley realized she was going to lose some of her precious moments with Hartley, because now it would be after nine o'clock when they returned. There was nothing she could do about it.

They walked up to the auditorium, slipped quietly through the door and silently joined the parents who were standing along one wall watching. It seemed to Shelley an exceptionally pretty party. The girls were all dressed in pastel cotton dresses and each was wearing a *lei* of pink carnations. The boys wore carnations in the buttonholes of their best suits. They were all very dignified as they danced around the auditorium to the music of a band of four high-school boys. Shelley located Katie dancing with a boy who was shorter than she was—so many of the boys were shorter than the girls Shelley thought Katie was having as good a time as it was possible to have with a short boy, but she could not be sure. Like all the girls Katie looked rather solemn. Not as solemn as the girls who were wearing their first high heels, but solemn for Katie. Shelley was glad to see that Katie's next partner, who had bushy hair, was taller. Katie's expression was one of elation suppressed by anxiety about not stepping on her partner's feet. Shelley was sure that this boy must be Rudy. Katie did not appear to recognize either Shelley or her relatives.

Eager not to miss any time with Hartley, Shelley glanced surreptitiously at her watch every thirty seconds and was glad when the party ended and Katie joined them.

"Did you have a good time?" Mavis asked.

"Oh, I guess so." Katie spoke coldly as they left the auditorium.

Shelley and Mrs. Stickney exchanged a glance. What had gone wrong? Shelley shivered in the cool night air. She should have worn a sweater.

Katie walked to the car in silence. She slid into the seat beside Shelley, filling the station wagon with the spicy fragrance of her carnation *lei*.

"What happened, dear?" Mavis asked.

"I was having a perfectly marvelous time and then you had to come along and spoil everything," Katie burst out.

"*Now* what have I done?" Mavis's voice was weary.

"You brought Shelley and Nana in and watched as if we were all a bunch of animals in a zoo or something," Katie accused her mother. "You spoiled everything."

"But there was nothing wrong with that," protested Mavis. "Other parents were watching, and I thought it was a very nice party. You girls looked lovely in your light dresses with your *leis*."

"I was the only one there with three people watching," said Katie. "And nobody who is anybody lets his parents come and watch anyway."

Of course, thought Shelley. She had felt exactly the same way at Katie's age about her mother's visiting

school. How well she remembered those arguments.
"But Shelley," her mother would say, "the board of
education wants parents to visit school and at P.T.A.
we are urged to visit." "I don't care, Mother," Shelley
would answer. "Nobody's mother visits school in the
eighth grade." Now she wished she had remembered
and somehow kept Mavis and her mother from watching the party. She could have made some excuse about
her date with Hartley and asked them to drive her
home. Now they were wasting precious minutes.

"Katie, that's ridiculous," said Mavis, inserting the
key into the ignition. "The parents pay for the series
of lessons and there is no reason why they shouldn't
see what their children are doing."

"Mommy, you don't *understand*," complained Katie.

"Katie, I wish you would stop saying that," snapped
Mavis, her patience at an end.

"I understand," said Mrs. Stickney. "What Katie is
really saying when she complains about our watching
is, 'I am trying to grow up—I want to be free of my
mother and grandmother and so I don't want them
watching me.' And what Mavis is saying is, 'Katie is
still my little girl and so I have a right to watch.' "

"I guess you are right, Mother." Mavis sounded
tired. "Children do have to grow up."

Everyone was silent as the station wagon traveled
up the main street. Why, of course, thought Shelley.
It was all as simple as that. That was all she and her
mother ever really argued about. She was trying to
grow up and her mother did not want to lose her
little girl. The argument might be disguised as a dis-
agreement about a slicker, or visiting school, or how
late she could stay out, but it always meant the same
thing. Shelley wanted to grow up and her mother felt
she was still her little girl. And that was the reason

she had stuffed the roses in the Disposall. She had been trying to say, *Now* I am going to grow up.

"I am at a very difficult stage," said Katie, in a voice that suggested everyone should sympathize with her problems.

"Not really?" said Mrs. Stickney, and laughed.

Shelley could see that Katie felt her grandmother was being most unsympathetic.

"Tell us about your difficult stage," suggested Mrs. Stickney.

"Well, I read an article—" Katie began defensively.

"She's read an article," chortled Mrs. Stickney. "And I suppose the article said a thirteen-year-old girl is going through a lot of difficult changes."

Mavis shared her mother's amusement. "It must have been that article that said a thirteen-year-old girl is half child, half woman."

"You don't have to make fun of me," Katie said crossly. "What I mean is I am not like Shelley, who doesn't have any problems."

"Why, I do, too," said Shelley, surprised at this view of herself. "Lots of them. I had a terrible time with biology."

"Oh, school." Katie was scornful. "School doesn't count. I mean you have dates and things."

"But school does count," protested Shelley. "It's terribly important. And just because I have dates doesn't mean they are always with the right boys."

"Don't you like Hartley?" asked Katie.

"Of course I like Hartley," said Shelley. "I mean . . . boys at home. And I have other problems, too."

"What?" asked Katie.

"Katie, do you think because you are thirteen you have all the problems?" Mavis asked.

"Well, the article said—" began Katie.

"I don't care what it said," snapped Mrs. Stickney. "Look at me. My hair is gray. I wear bifocals. I have bridgework. All because I have changed."

"But you're . . . grown-up," Katie pointed out, hesitating just enough so that Shelley knew she had been about to say, "But you are old."

"Katie, just because a girl grows up doesn't mean she stops feeling," Mavis pointed out.

"And take your mother," said Mrs. Stickney. "Her life is difficult too. Her children are growing up whether she wants them to or not. She will have to let Luke ride his motorcycle whether she wants to or not. And probably the hardest part of all is having a daughter too old to read *Winnie-the-Pooh* but young enough to misinterpret articles in women's magazines. That is a terrible stage for a mother to go through. I don't know why someone doesn't write an article about it." Mrs. Stickney and her daughter both thought this was extremely funny.

"I never read *Winnie-the-Pooh*. Mommy read it to me," said Katie grumpily. "Why does this family have to argue all the time?"

"Yes, for goodness' sake, let's stop arguing," said Mavis. "Let's get Shelley home for her date with Hartley, and then the rest of us can go downtown for an ice-cream soda."

"I'm starved," said Katie, as they turned into the driveway behind Hartley's parked car.

"Mavis, I've been meaning to tell you—I think you're putting on a little weight," said Mrs. Stickney. "Don't you think you should cut out desserts?"

"Mother, you say that every time you come to visit us," answered Mavis. "I think I am old enough to know what I should eat."

Shelley stifled a desire to laugh as she climbed out of the station wagon. She found Hartley in the garage examining the motorcycle and talking to Tom and

Luke. "Hi," she said, feeling the pang she had felt so often lately. This was her next-to-the-last date with Hartley. "The others have gone downtown for a soda."

"That's a good idea," said Hartley. "Why don't we go for a ride and then stop in for a soda?"

"I'd love to," agreed Shelley. "Wait till I get my sweater."

She ran upstairs and as she turned on the light in her room, her glance fell on the unfinished letter on her desk. She picked it up and read it over before she crumpled it into a ball and tossed it into the wastebasket. How silly she had been to be so indignant over nothing. All her mother really meant by her letter was that she loved Shelley. And all Shelley's answer meant was that she wanted to grow up. And she would grow up, was growing up every day. There was nothing her mother could do but accept it and there was nothing Shelley could do but try to understand her mother's feelings. Maybe neither of them would do a very good job but it would all turn out all right, she was sure.

Shelley pulled her sweater out of the drawer and with a light heart ran down the steps to meet Hartley.

Chapter 16

The moment Shelley awoke she knew there was something different about this day. It took her a moment to remember what the difference was and then it came to her—this was the last day of school, the last time she would see Hartley. Tomorrow her mother and father would arrive to take her home. She lay in bed a few moments looking around her room. The Japanese prints, the gilded flatirons that had held her books, the India print bedspread, the window sills a few inches above the floor—all this she must remember always.

Shelley lingered in the bathroom, taking in the names on the adhesive tape over the towel racks (how surprised she had been that first day to see seven towel racks in one bathroom), the hamper still left open for the cat, the rough white towels bearing the names of schools. These, too, she would remember.

Breakfast at the painted table in the dining room with the linoleum floor was to be stored away in Shelley's memory too. Shelley smiled as she helped herself to a piece of brittle toast made under the broiler. Before she had lived with the Michies she had thought that pop-up toasters and rugs on the dining-room floor were necessities. Now she knew they were not. Mavis would rather work at her potter's wheel than vacuum a dining-room rug. Toast for a family could be made more quickly under the broiler. It tasted better, too. It was toasted all the way through and not just on the outside.

"I just love the last day of school," said Katie with a sigh, as she sprinkled sugar over her oatmeal. "Half-hour classes are fun and we don't have to learn a thing. And this afternoon I am going to take my cooking notebook out to the incinerator and burn it!"

"You'll do no such thing!" said Mavis sharply. "There are some excellent recipes in your notebook."

"But it is my notebook," protested Katie.

"I don't care if it is," said Mavis. "I would like to use the recipes even if you don't."

Katie's expression showed that her mother always spoiled all her fun. Shelley smiled to herself. The same old mother-daughter tug of war.

"Katie thinks everything should be made out of a mix," Luke told his grandmother.

" 'Mother, they've crowned me Queen of the May exclamation point,' " said Katie, to no one in particular.

"You keep quiet!" ordered Luke.

The Michies' day was starting normally. Shelley left the house early so that she could enjoy a leisurely walk through the sunshine to school. The groves were now bearing oranges the size of peas, and the pomegranate tree was covered with brilliant tangerine-colored blossoms. It was strange the way California flowers were so often gaudy. Slowly Shelley walked up the steps of San Sebastian Union High School. She would never walk up those steps again, only down.

The halls were filled with an atmosphere of excitement. Everyone was chattering, laughing, signing one another's yearbooks, making plans for the summer. Shelley was once more an outsider just as she had been the first day of school. She could not share any plans for the summer or the next year. She could only say good-by.

With her receipt in hand she went to the office of the yearbook to pick up her copy of the *Argonaut*. Then she, too, was swept into the crowd writing in one another's yearbooks. This was her last day and she was going to enjoy every minute of it. At San Sebastian, she soon discovered, it was the custom to write a message instead of merely signing a name. "It's been fun knowing you," Shelley wrote in one yearbook after another. The more important the relationship between students, the longer the message was supposed to be.

It was during the first period that report cards were handed out. As Shelley held the envelope in her hand she was confident of the B in biology that would assure her of a C for the year. All her quiz grades had been high and she had taken such pains with the drawings in her notebook that she was sure even Mr. Ericson could not criticize them. She pulled out the cards and read her grades. A in English, A in journalism, B in history (those "why" questions always bothered her), A in Latin, C in physical education. Ah, here it was. Biology—B for two semesters. B for both semesters! Darling Mr. Ericson! Bless his heart, he wasn't so bad after all. She only hoped he had been as generous with Philip.

"Good news?" Hartley asked.

"B for both semesters of biology!" said Shelley. "That was more than Mr. Ericson promised me."

"Good for Mr. Ericson!" said Hartley enthusiastically. "But I'm sure you deserved it. You worked hard."

"Here, Hartley, write in my yearbook," said Shelley, holding out her pen.

Hartley shook his head. "Tonight. I need more time to write in your book."

"All right," Shelley's eyes lingered on Hartley's face. She wondered what he would write and what she would find to say to him. If only she did not have to say good-by. . . .

Few teachers made any attempt at teaching that last day of school. The English teacher made suggestions for summer reading. Mrs. Boyce, in journalism, read aloud a few examples of good reporting from the morning paper while the class passed *Argonauts* back and forth.

In biology Mr. Ericson looked sardonically at his furiously autographing class and said nothing at all. Shelley approached him and said, "Mr. Ericson, I want to thank you for the B for two semesters. I only expected a C."

Mr. Ericson smiled—a very nice smile for Mr. Ericson. "You deserved it, Shelley. You did excellent work when you finally settled down."

"Thank you," replied Shelley. He was the same old Mr. Ericson. He could not leave out that remark about finally settling down. Not Mr. Ericson. But in spite of her annoyance, Shelley was grateful to him. Now she did not need to worry about a laboratory science in college, where she wanted to study botany because she had always been interested in plants.

Back at her table Frisbie thrust his *Argonaut* into her hands and helped himself to hers. She read hi scrawled message when he returned the book to he "Hi, Webfoot— Remember the night we burned hay? Friz." Shelley laughed. She certainly woul member that night. Always. It was one of her hap memories.

She turned to Philip and wondered if she ask about his grade.

"I got a C," Philip confided without her asking.

"Oh, Philip," Shelley exclaimed. "I'm so glad!"

"Yes, that's a load off my mind," admitted Philip. "Now I can repeat the first semester next year." He pushed his *Argonaut* toward her.

Smiling, Shelley opened the book while she remembered the Ping-Pong games, the rainy afternoon he had almost kissed her, the night they had all carried the hay out to the incinerator. She was not sorry she had liked Philip—she only regretted that she had not understood much sooner that he was not the boy she wanted him to be. She watched him bending over her yearbook and noticed that the sunburned patch had appeared on his nose once more. "Dear Philip," she wrote slowly, trying to think of some reference she could make to the dates she had shared with him. "I am very glad I knew you. You helped make my year in San Sebastian complete. I hope you and Jeannie have fun this summer. Shelley."

Shelley exchanged *Argonauts* with Philip and opened her copy to his message. "Dear Shelley," he had written. "You are the gamest Ping-Pong player I have ever known. Good luck. Phil."

"I guess you could say I play a game game even if I can't play a good game," Shelley said. Philip was looking at her quite seriously. She returned his look for a moment and then, with a smile tinged with sadness, she took her eyes from his face. He, too, was remembering the painful experience they had shared, n experience that neither of them would ever forget, cause it had been painful.

'Next," said Jeannie, trading books with Shelley, saw her glance quickly at the words Philip had written.

en the two girls took back their own books, read Jeannie's note. "Dear Shelley," it began,

"I have really enjoyed knowing you. It has been fun to share a table in biology and to eat lunch out on the lawn with such a wide-eyed innocent. Please stay that way always. I wish I were leaving San Sebastian too, but since I am not, please let's stay friends. We can write and sometime, someplace we are sure to meet again. I'll miss you terribly. With love, Jeannie."

Shelley faced Jeannie across the table, which they now had to themselves because the boys had drifted off to sign more books. "What do you mean, 'wide-eyed innocent'?" she asked curiously.

"Well, you are," said Jeannie seriously. "That's why I like you. You really think it is fun to do the most ordinary things and because you had fun, I had fun too. You know. Things like eating lunch out of a paper bag."

"But it was fun," said Shelley.

"Yes, it was when I looked at things the way you do, as if everything were new and exciting," agreed Jeannie thoughtfully. "I guess my trouble is that I have always lived in San Sebastian and I understand some things you don't. Like the way a lot of girls dash out to the gym and put their gym blouses on over their dresses to show that they were just too, too busy to remember ahead of time that this was the day of the football game."

"Is that the way it really is?" Shelley asked, only half believing.

"Yes," said Jeannie. "You didn't even see things like that, and you walked right into school and made the most sought-after boy like you. I really admired you for that. I've wanted to date Philip since I was in junior high school."

"And now you are," said Shelley.

"Yes." Jeannie's face was alive with happiness. "But you know, I don't suppose he would ever have looked at me if I hadn't been the friend of a new girl. I was always just someone who had always been around. You know. Part of the scenery or something."

"But you could help him in biology and I couldn't," Shelley pointed out.

"That helped," admitted Jeannie, flashing her old mischievous smile, which always reminded Shelley of a bright-eyed sparrow.

The last bell rang, and Shelley and Jeannie walked out of the building together. "My last time down these steps," remarked Shelley, as they emerged into the sunshine with their yearbooks in the crooks of their arms. They walked out to the sidewalk in silence and faced one another in the shade of one of the grevillea trees that lined the main street, a tree that was covered with blossoms like strips of orange fringe.

"I guess this is good-by," said Jeannie. "Remember what I said. Don't ever change."

"It is only good-by for now," said Shelley. "Really it is."

The girls parted quickly, Shelley walking toward the orange groves, and Jeannie toward the little house behind the dusty pampas grass. It was sweet of Jeannie to want Shelley to stay as she was, but she would change, of course. Everyone did. She had changed this year, but perhaps in the way Jeannie meant she would not change. Perhaps she could go home and continue to look at the world as if it were a new and exciting place. Remembering the ragged palms of San Sebastian would make the cool green firs that she had always taken for granted seem remarkable, something to look at as if she were seeing them for the first time.

The pomegranate tree reminded Shelley with a pang of Hartley. Her good-by to Jeannie had been good-by for now, but it was different with a boy. They would say good-by too, and he would write and she would write. Then he would meet another girl, she would meet another boy, they would forget to write and that would be the end.

Shelley bit her lip. She did not want this to be the end with Hartley. She was not ready yet. He was too dear to her. Everything about him was dear—his dark eyes, the way they were both amused at the same things, that something about him that made her want to talk to him, the way she never worried about their next date.

I'm in love, thought Shelley suddenly. She was in love with Hartley and everything was happening too fast. She wasn't even sure she was ready to be in love, but there it was and there was nothing she could do about it but say good-by. She was not ready for that, either. It had all happened too quickly. She had had so little time with Hartley, she had wasted so many precious months. Shelley walked slowly through the opening in the privet hedge, which brushed against her arms because it needed pruning. Tonight the boy she loved would walk out through the hedge and she would never see him again.

Shelley spent the afternoon packing her trunk. It was good to have something definite to do. She tried not to think, but each garment that she folded had associations for her—the dress she had worn the first day of school, the skirt she had worn picnicking in the mountains with Hartley, the pink raincoat she had not minded wearing after all.

Katie sat cross-legged on the bed, watching and chattering. Shelley was glad to have her because she helped hold off the moment that lay ahead.

"Guess what?" Katie asked. "Rudy's mother is having a supper party for his birthday and I'm invited and Pamela isn't!"

Shelley wrapped paper around the galoshes she

had never worn at all and tucked them into the corner of her trunk. "And you're glad your best friend isn't invited?" she asked.

"She isn't my best friend any more." Katie was emphatic. "Not after what she did at the dancing-class party."

"What did she do?" asked Shelley.

"Well, one of the dances was girls' choice," Katie began. "The dancing teacher gave each girl a carnation, and she was supposed to pin it on the lapel of the boy she wanted to dance with. It is a rule that we are supposed to walk, not run, across the auditorium to ask a boy to dance. The teacher says walking means we have to keep one foot on the floor at all times. Well, Pamela cheated. She ran. I saw her. She got to Rudy first and she knew all the time I had planned to ask him."

"But didn't you have the last dance with him when we watched that night?" asked Shelley, raising her voice because Luke had started to ride his motorcycle around the house.

"Yes, and he said he liked my hair." Katie was obviously pleased with herself. "And it was boys' choice, too. For the last dance. The last dance is important, isn't it?"

"It certainly is," Shelley reassured her. "The most important of all."

Katie unfolded her legs, rose from the bed and walked across the room to the dresser, where she propped her chin on her fists and stared thoughtfully at herself in the mirror.

"You're getting prettier," Shelley told her.

"Do you really think so?" Katie turned around. "Do you think there is hope after all?"

"I sure do," said Shelley.

Katie sighed happily. Then she said, "Tonight is your last date with Hartley, isn't it?"

"Yes, it is." The pang came back to Shelley.

"How can you bear to say good-by to him?" asked Katie.

"Oh, I'll manage," Shelley said airily, but how she would manage she did not know. It hurt to think about it.

Supper was lively and that helped. Luke said he liked his carrots cut crosswise in circles, instead of lengthwise in strips the way his mother cooked them. Mavis said she thought they had more flavor when they were cut lengthwise. Mrs. Stickney said she thought they looked more attractive when cut in circles. Tom said carrots were carrots no matter how you cut them. Katie said her cooking teacher, that old sourpuss, said they should be cut lengthwise but Katie did not know why.

Shelley settled the argument. She said that in biology they had looked at sections of carrot under the microscope and had seen that the cells were long and thin. If carrots were cut in circles, more cells would be cut through than if the carrots were cut lengthwise and more flavor would run out into the cooking water. Luke and Katie were impressed by this display of knowledge. Why, I have *used* my biology, marveled Shelley.

And then the moment arrived that Shelley both anticipated and dreaded. Hartley twirled the doorbell.

It was a funny thing about that evening. Shelley had the feeling that because they would not see one another again they should say something memorable or that something momentous should happen. It was not that way at all.

"Let's take our *Argonauts* over to Vincente and

write in them over a plate of doughnut holes," Hartley suggested. It might have been any date.

"All right," agreed Shelley. It did not really matter what they did so long as they were together. Shelley had little to say. She looked at everything they passed on the road to Vincente—the Giant Orange, the olive groves, the "Rain for Rent" sign that she had once thought so strange, the river that really had been filled with water during the winter and was now drying up once more, and thought how unreal it had all seemed that day she had stepped out of the plane.

"Hartley!" said Shelley suddenly. "Do you mind if we don't eat doughnut holes tonight? There is something I have always wanted to do."

"What?" asked Hartley.

"Stop at the Giant Orange," answered Shelley. "That is one of the native customs I haven't tried."

Hartley laughed. "Whatever you say," he said, and turned into a driveway to back the car around and head toward San Sebastian once more. "I guess the Giant Orange is a pretty typical sight in the hotter parts of California but I never thought of it as being unusual." Hartley drove up beside the orange-juice stand built in the shape of an orange, and ordered two large glasses of orange juice from the girl inside. Shelley watched while she squeezed the oranges in an electric juicer, dipped a scoop of crushed ice into each glass, handed over a tray that fastened to the car door and set two glasses of foaming orange juice on it. Hartley paid for the orange juice and while Shelley steadied the glasses, drove the car a few feet from the stand to leave room for the next car that stopped. They each took a glass of orange juice.

"To our futures," said Hartley.

"To our futures," repeated Shelley gravely. Their

separate futures. The orange juice was cold and sweet. Shelley and Hartley smiled at one another in the dim light of a bulb on the outside of the Giant Orange, but they did not talk. It was the first time they had ever been at a loss for something to say.

"Is there enough light for you to write in my *Argonaut?*" Hartley asked, when they had finished their orange juice.

"Yes." Shelley handed her yearbook to Hartley and picked up her pen. She turned the pages of his book, looking for a large empty space to write in, and when she found one she sat nibbling the end of her pen and thinking. Now that the time had come, she did not know what to write to Hartley. She could list all the good times they had had together (but not nearly enough), but why do that? She would not forget and neither would he. She could try to tell him how much he meant to her, but somehow she did not know the words to use. She could try to tell him how much she would miss him, but that would be painful to write. She glanced at Hartley, who was writing on the last page of her yearbook. He looked serious, as if what he was doing was not something to be taken lightly.

Shelley knew then the words she wanted to use. She uncapped her pen and wrote quickly. "Dear Hartley," she began. "It took me a while to find it out, but you are the boy I have always wanted to meet. I am sorry to say good-by so soon. With love, Shelley." She had not needed a large space after all. She blew gently on the words, because she did not have a blotter, and closed the book. She had written only a few words but Hartley would understand how much those words meant. That was the most wonderful thing about Hartley. He understood.

Hartley returned her book to her and when she started to open it he said brusquely, "Read it later," and started the car. Hartley drove slowly back to San Sebastian. It seemed a strange sort of date, driving out of town for a glass of orange juice and coming right home again; but somehow, there seemed nothing else to do. Hartley turned into the Michies' driveway, stopped the car, and turned off the lights. The moment Shelley had been dreading with that awful aching dread had arrived. They had to say good-by.

Hartley got out of the car, walked around and opened the door for her. Hand in hand they walked across the lawn to the front door. The night was rich with the fragrance of lemon blossoms and honeysuckle. "Shelley," Hartley said softly. "Let's say good-by quickly."

"Yes," whispered Shelley, clinging to her *Argonaut* as her eyes searched the darkness for his face.

Hartley brushed back her hair, put his hands on either side of her face, leaned over, and kissed her gently on the lips. "Good-by, Shelley," he whispered.

"Good-by." Shelley's voice was faint.

And then Hartley was gone. Shelley went into the dark house and closed the door quietly behind her. It was all over. She tiptoed up the creaky stairs and into her room, where she turned on the light and sat numbly down on the bed. Her *Argonaut*, she discovered, was still in her hands. She opened it slowly and with awkward fingers turned to the page that carried Hartley's words.

His handwriting was firm and sure. "Dear Shelley," he had written. "There is so much that I could say to you. I could begin with the day you walked into that classroom looking eager and a little frightened. I could write about the wonderful way you have of looking as if you thought something exciting was about to happen—but why write these things? It all means just one thing. I love you, Shelley. I really do. And now—good-by. Hartley."

Shelley sat there on her bed with her yearbook on her lap, and her eyes were filled with tears. This was love, she knew. Not the love-for-keeps that would come later, but love that was real and true just the same. She heard Katie's familiar knock at her door (the last time, perhaps) and blinked her eyes to try to force back the tears.

Katie entered wearing her terry-cloth bathrobe. "Shelley," she began and stopped. "Shelley—" Her voice was anxious. "Is something wrong?"

Shelley shook her head. She could not speak.

Understanding seemed to dawn on Katie's face. "Are you—you're not heartbroken, are you?"

Shelley shook her head again and managed a shaky laugh.

"Oh, Shelley." Katie sat down on the bed. She looked both anxious and frightened.

"It's all right, Katie." Shelley had to reassure her. "It was just sort of—hard to say good-by."

"Then I never want to say good-by to a boy," said Katie flatly.

"Oh, no, Katie." Shelley was finding it easier to talk. "Please don't feel that way. You'll have to say good-by sometime, you know. Everybody does."

"But if it makes you unhappy—" protested Katie.

"Not really unhappy." Shelley had to make Katie understand. "Just sorry because I have to say good-by. It's all right, Katie. Really it is." She was silent a moment, thinking. "I guess that's what growing up is. Saying good-by to a lot of things. Sometimes it is easy and sometimes it isn't. But it is all right."

"I am glad you don't have a broken heart." Katie looked relieved and a little puzzled. "Well, I guess

I'd better go to bed or Dad will be yelling at me," she said reluctantly.

"Good night, Katie." Shelley was smiling. She was going to miss Katie.

When Katie had gone Shelley sat on her bed turning over in her mind what she had just told her. Someday Katie would understand. Then, filled with restlessness, she crossed to the window and looked out into the night. She felt as if she had to do something to relieve her pent-up feelings. She slipped out of her room and down the stairs, avoiding the creakiest steps, and out of the house. She crossed the driveway, seized the rope that hung from the top of the eucalyptus tree, and climbed to the top of the child's slide. She stood poised a moment before she grasped the ring and pushed off, swinging out through the night, past the trunks of the eucalyptus trees, out over the road with her hair blowing back from her face and her skirts flying behind her. The night air was soft on her skin and the stars seemed close enough to touch. Shelley was happy, happier than she had ever been in her life.

Above her in the eucalyptus trees the cry of the doves was sad and sweet.